BLIND TO THE EYE

DEANNA SANDERS

PUBLISHED BY BAM! PUBLISHING

Blind To the Eye

2nd Edition

Print edition ISBN: 9781631114434

Printed in the United States of America

TABLE OF CONTENTS

Blind To The Eye

By: DeAnna Sanders

Dedication:

I want to thank my parents for encouraging me and always being there for me. Also, I will have to give a special thanks to my biggest critic and supporter, my sister (Shon). Thank you for pushing me towards my dreams and please continue to push. It is helping me to continue to go farther and excel higher. One more thanks to my Auntie (Debra) who also encouraged me and gave me an idea on how to pursue my writing and book career.

�

CHAPTER 1

As I gazed outside from the window of which will soon no longer be my home, I see a familiar face walking into the building. I started to gather my stuff together as I wasn't sure who it was, but I had a feeling that they came for me. I heard the rattling of keys against the door as the nurse unlocked it. As the door was opening I could see the face in which I was unsure of whom it was I saw. I knew that face looked familiar. The face of my childhood friend, Stan. "Hey Kait." Stan said as he walked in. He could tell that I looked shocked to see him. "Hi, Stan. Where's Cassandra?" I said looking totally confused. "Well, you know your mom can't stand to see you in this place. So, she asked if I would come and get you and of course I don't mind at all. Now, stop asking me all these questions and let's get the hell outta this crazy house. I'm starving." I saw that he forgot already where he was as he quickly put his hand over his mouth hoping that the nurse would forgive him for what he just said. "Aww man I'm sorry I didn't mean to say that out loud." I shook my head in agreement as I followed behind him. To hear him say that he was hungry wasn't really a big secret, he was always ready to stuff his face.

As we were walking down the steps, I could feel him staring at me from the corner of my eye. "What the hell are you looking at?" I said without looking his way. "Nothing. You look good." I stopped immediately as he was pointing to which car was his. "What?" Stan said with a blank look. "Did you really just say that? Really? I've been in a damn crazy house for the past 3 years without any makeup, pedicure, manicure, hair stylist, eyebrows looking a mess...you know what let me stop! " Stan knew that when I got mad I could go on and on without stopping or taking a breath. He took responsibility for his actions. "Kait, I'm sorry. I haven't seen you in a while and no matter what you think, in my eyes, you were always perfect." I rolled my eyes at him as he closed my door to his brand new Benz. The car had that new car smell that made you wanna stay in it all the time. "New car?" I questioned Stan as he started the engine. "Um...kind of I bought it like 2 months ago. You like?" Stan knew I've always liked the Mercedes and for him to buy one? What an ass. "It's okay, I would have gotten a different interior color, but it's cool." I couldn't let Stan know that I was envious of his car. "So are you going to tell me the real reason why Cassandra didn't wanna come pick me up?" I said as I was looking at the asylum as it disappeared behind me through the side mirror. "Why do you do that?" He asked. "Do what?" I replied. "Call your mom Cassandra." It took me a second to think of an answer as I really didn't care to respond. "Because that's her name." I said still looking out of the side mirror. "Well, you hurt her feelings when you call her that instead of mom. I don't know what the hell happened between ya'll, but she raised you and it's disrespectful." I looked at Stan with the most devilish look as he was driving. "The hell with Cassandra and the hell with you." I told him as his thought of respect was to any woman who openly gave him some ass. "Kait, you....you....you are something else." I knew he had nothing else left to say as he know I will always have the last words. "Hey, you missed my exit." I was pointing at the exit sign towards my apartment at this time. "Oh, yeah I forgot to tell you." He said as he was rubbing his bald head in forgetfulness. "Tell me what?" I shouted angrily as if I didn't already know the answer. "Your mom got rid of your apartment. She wants ya'll to get closer and plus considering the situation I think that it would be best." I didn't say anything because I knew that she always got her way even if it was in the wrong way.

My adoptive parents pretty much owned the small town of Baton Rouge, LA. Well, my adoptive father anyway, Cassandra is just married to Eric. I know that I am supposed to love and care for the people who took me out of foster care and gave me a home, but I can't stand them. It's not because he's black and she's white they aren't my real parents. We just don't agree at all about my future. They want me to go into the family business of Law. I know it's probably selfish to just think about myself and maybe even a little ungrateful that I have parents who are willing to give me anything I want, but for some reason that's not me. I like to work for what's mine so that I don't have to worry about anyone coming to take it within a blink of an eye.

I started frowning at Stan as we were pulling into the driveway. "Now, no cussing, no fighting, be polite and nice. Understand?" I looked around and around throughout the car as he was saying this bull to me. "What are you looking for?" He said to me with confusion. "I'm looking for the person you are talking to because it sure as hell isn't me." I said back to him. "Just be nice okay. For me please?" I hated it when Stan used the phrase "for me" he knew that when he did it I couldn't say no. "Fine Stan, but if she starts anything with me I'm not gonna be nice." He smiled with relief hoping that I would be on my best behavior. The house still looks the same, I said to myself as I got out the car. "I'll get your bags while you go on in." I looked at Stan in shock because he was trying to be a gentlemen today.

As I reached for the door knob it opened before I could even get my hand on it. "SURPRISE! Welcome home Kaitlyn." I jumped back as I heard the loud different voices screaming at me when I stepped into the house. A welcome home party wasn't something that I expected Cassandra to do. "I wanted to do something special for you and wanted you to know how much I love you, not just me but everyone in this room loves you." Cassandra said. I could see that everyone was waiting for me to say something. I wasn't shy or afraid to say anything back I just didn't know what they might be expecting me to say; a big speech or just a few words.

"Well, this is a big surprise." I stated as I rubbed my hand against my pants thigh hoping to get some of the sweat off. "I wasn't expecting a party for me. I'm glad to see everyone and thank you for being here and......" I paused for a while debating whether to say that I loved them back. I swallowed in order to build the words together and replied with a small smile, "I love you mom and everyone here." I could tell that made her happy to hear me call her mom. "Aww, Kaitlyn we love you too, we all do." Cassandra's mother smiled through her tears as she looked like she been cutting onions with big raindrops of tears rolling down her face.

After all of the hugging, crying, talking, and laughing, with Cassandra and relatives, it was finally time to eat some grub. I can't even tell you how much I missed a good home cooked meal. We had everything you could possibly name on the table. It was almost like Thanksgiving, but in the spring time. "Boy, Kait I don't care what they say about your mama." Stan said to me as he was feeding his face. "What's that?" I said to Stan with a smirk on my face because he was making me be nice by calling her mom. "Your mom may be white, but she has a black person's soul. Just taste the chicken and you'll understand what I'm saying." Everyone laughed in agreement with him stating that fact. I nodded my head as well. I may have not liked her as a person, but she really could cook.

I waved goodnight to my relatives with a forced smile as I was sitting on the porch swing. Cassandra was walking towards me as she was waving goodbye as well. "Did you enjoy yourself?" Cassandra asked and my reply was just a nod. "Did you enjoy spending time with family?" Again, I am not related to none of these people, why does she insist on acting like I really belong here? "Kaitlyn, I wished you would just answer me and not give me the silent treatment." I looked at her with a nonchalant face and said, "I just want to enjoy my first day of freedom in peace." Before I knew it I had replied with such an attitude. It wasn't my intention to make her feel as if I wasn't thankful. I saw how my words changed her mood so I quickly made a comeback. "I'm sorry. I didn't mean to get angry, of course I enjoyed everyone." I said apologetically to Cassandra. "It's ok, I know you didn't mean it. You've had a rough time. Ever since you........." I could tell she had to catch herself before saying anything else. "It's kind of chilly out here and I know you hate the cold so I'm gonna stay out here for a little while longer." I said to her as I didn't want her to get the wrong idea that we were best friends now. "Okay." She said as she kissed me on my forehead before going back in to the house. Eww, did she really just put her lips on me? I immediately became disgusted.

Finally, peace and quiet so I thought. "Move over big duke." Stan motioned as he had been sitting in his car talking on the phone for the longest. "I'm trying to relax here. Why don't you take yo ass home?" I told him with aggravation. "I can't go home, not just yet. You know I gotta poke and pick at you." I rolled my eyes as I slowly moved over to let Stan sit next to me. "So who where you on the phone with for almost a decade?" I inquired of him as I could really care less about who he was talking to. "Jealous are we? I knew it, I knew it." He said as he was rubbing his broad chest. "What the hell are you whining about now? You don't know nothing." I assured him as he was now caressing and not rubbing his chest anymore. "Kait, I knew you would come around after all these years and realized what you were missing." Before I could catch myself I had let out a big hysterical laugh. I was laughing so hard that a tear came down my eye. "I'm sorry, but ya not my type at all." I said as I was still chuckling. "Like hell. Look at this sexy bald head, these 6 pack abs, these arms. No one can resist Stan the man." Again, I had let out a big laugh as his quote for getting girls was, "Stan the man." "Please, boy, the only girls who can't resist you are hood rats and chicken heads." I used a form of sign language relating to a chicken with my hands so he would get the picture. We were rambling on and on not realizing how late it was getting. It felt good to have someone there that understood me. Even though he was older than me by a year, he always felt like he was the boss of me. I've known Stan since middle school and it didn't help that he was my next door neighbor because he was always over. But, I loved having him as my buddy. He has been my shoulder to cry on, my ears to listen, and my protector. It's almost as if he was my personal angel sent to protect me.

I was sitting trying to listen to Stan, but my mind started to wonder off. My mind had went back to my childhood which was something I kept blocked. I couldn't understand why this happened to me and not anyone else. Not even Stan knows. Even if he did know he never mentioned it or made notation that he knew. I wondered why it happened to me or what I could have done differently to prevent it. As I grew silent, I felt some sort of discomfort in my chest. I wasn't sure what it was I just knew that it was hurting me. I rubbed my hands across my face and felt the wetness in which I thought it was raining, but in reality I was crying. The tightness in my chest was still there, but it started to ease up as I felt a firmness of warmth wrapped around me. "What's wrong, Kait?" Stan whispered to me with concern as he rubbed my back gently to calm me down. "Nothing, it's nothing." I said as I wiped my eyes swiftly with my hands. "Well, it doesn't seem like nothing. You went from laughing and talking to crying in just seconds. C'mon, you know you can talk to me about anything." I looked at him and could tell he was genuine with his words. "I can't tell you, I just can't." I shook my head and stood up as I was ready for him to stop questioning me. "Why? We've never kept secrets from each other. We've always shared everything with each other. The good, the bad, the happy and the sad. So, don't lie to me and say that it's nothing." He said. "STAN! Just leave it alone okay. PLEASE!" I replied back in a very angry tone. At this time Cassandra had made her way to the porch looking concerned about me, but disappointed towards Stan. "Stanley, it's been a long day. I think you should go home now and try to visit another time, okay?" She said to him. "I'm sorry, Kait. I didn't mean to make you upset. Mrs. Thomas I apologize to you also for disturbing your home." I could tell by the look in his eyes as he walked towards his car that he was truly sorry, but at the same time I knew our conversation wasn't over.

As the night carried on, I was ready to get a good night's sleep. I was heading upstairs to my bedroom until I heard footsteps walking through the hallway in my direction. "You know your father wanted to be here, but he still feels like he has to be at the office all the time even after retirement." She stated as if I really cared if that bastard was here or not. "Whatever." At this point my response went back to simple words or simple gestures. "Hey?" I turned around and said to her before heading to my room. "Yes?" Cassandra said. "Why didn't you come and visit me?" I asked. She stared at me with the look on her face as if I knew the answer to that question already. "Kait, I just didn't want to see you like that. I wanted you to get better so that you could come home." Even though her answer wasn't what I wanted I agreed with a nod again and continued towards my old room.

It felt good to be out of that place and in a home, but this wasn't a happy home. In fact this place is much worse than the crazy house. I knew if I stayed here it would only cause problems between me and Eric. He and I never really got along since day one. I ask myself all the time, "Why did I have to get adopted by this family?" My question was never answered, and I was still left feeling miserable, but I wasn't gonna look at the past and have a pity party. I was going to focus on the future and make sure that my kindness isn't taken as a weakness anymore.

CHAPTER 2

I could feel the brightness of the sun shining down on me as I was walking on the soft green grass. It was such a pretty day; the birds were chirping and the butterflies were flapping their bright colored wings. Before I could take another deep breath to inhale this beautiful sunny day, it suddenly became dark. I looked up at the sky to try and see what happened to the sun, but I couldn't see anything. Also, there was no one else outside but me; this was very strange. This was scary so I ran into the house as fast as I could and locked the door behind me. As I was leaning up against the door, I thought I heard a knock. I started walking towards the steps just thinking it was in my head until I heard two knocks again. I wasn't sure who was knocking because I didn't see anyone outside. So, I just ignored it and started walking up the steps. Before I could make it any further I heard a loud BOOM behind me. I was scared to see what it was, but I couldn't resist the temptation. I turned around and saw a dark shadowy figure. I couldn't tell if it was a person, yet alone a human. I could see this figure coming towards me so I ran as fast as - I could up the steps hoping that I could get away.

As I reached the top step, it grabbed and pulled me down. I was face to face with this creature now. It looked at me with hell in its eyes feeling satisfied that it had captured me. I wanted to scream, I wanted to run, I wanted to fight back, but nothing. The shadowy figure then pulled back and raised its hands in a charging form, the floor started to shake. The shake got harder, harder and harder. "WAKE UP, Kaitlyn! C'mon baby wake up! Kaitlyn! Kaitlyn!" I heard labored screaming in my ears. When I realized that I was looking at Cassandra, I let out a deep breath of relief and realized it was only a dream.

I didn't sleep worth crap last night. I really wanted to stay in bed all day, but I knew that wasn't going to happen. I heard a knock at my door as I knew who it was already. "Come in." I stated as I knew it was Cassandra. "Hey, how are you doing this morning?" A deep voice said. To my surprise it was Eric. "Oh, I'm doing okay." I said still feeling restless. "You know I wanted to be here when you got home, but there was a few emergencies that had to be taken care of at the office." He said. "Eric, you don't have to explain anything to me. You're grown." I said with a hint of cynicism "Kaitlyn, I don't want this to be unpleasant, okay. Now upon your release, the doctor put me and your mother in charge. So, I want nothing but respect from you." He said with a stern tone. Are you serious right now? Did he really just say that? "Well, I'll just move out so I won't have to abide by YOUR RULES." I replied back hard-heartedly. "Kaitlyn, you don't get it do you? C'mon you're not that stupid." Do you see what I mean by him being a bastard? At this point I was done talking to him. "You're not stable. Until the doctor declares you mentally stable, you're not allowed to live on your own considering the reason why you went there in the first place." He was unsympathetic with his words. "Eric!" Cassandra shouted. I don't know how long she had been standing there listening, but obviously long enough. The entire conversation quickly ended after Casandra interrupted. Sorry to say, but I was kind of glad she walked in when she did.

I started walking downstairs and I could hear Cassandra and Eric talking softly. They must have heard me coming down because while I was entering into the kitchen the whispering stopped. "Good Morning, how are you?" Cassandra asked as she was hoping I didn't over hear their conversation. "Okay, I guess." I replied. There was a few minutes of silence before more drama got started. "We think that you should continue to see a therapist." Eric said in between sips of coffee. I took a moment before I opened my mouth. "Um, I don't think I need to, but I will think about it." I told him. "Well, we don't want to pressure you, but we just think that it'll be a good idea. Your mom told me you had a nightmare last night." He answered as if he was trying to be so concerned. Ugh, please I need to get outta here. I couldn't believe he was trying to pretend that we were cool after the stunt he pulled earlier. Where are you, Stan? I wondered to myself. I called his ass like forty five minutes ago and he still wasn't there. "Like I said before, I will think about it." I replied matter-of-factly. The conversation was interrupted by the doorbell. "I'll get it."

Cassandra said as she gave Eric an evil glare. I heard Stan loud mouth as he was asking how she was doing and apologized again for upsetting me last night. Boy, I tell you if they only knew the real Stan I guarantee you they wouldn't be this nice to him. "Good Morning, Mr. Thomas." Stan said. "Good Morning, Stanley. Have you decided on which team you going with?" Eric asked as he was now reading the newspaper. "No, not yet sir, and you know I couldn't tell you that. My agent would kill me." Stan said with a chuckle. I stood in the doorway motioning him to come on as I had enough of listening to them telling me what I needed to do. "Nice to see you guys again." Stan said as he was trailing behind me. "Stanley wait." Eric said. "Listen, watch her okay. You know her situation so if she looks or feels uncomfortable with something I want you to call us as soon as possible okay." Eric said flatly while still trying to pretend to be concerned. "Sure, Mr. Thomas." I could hear their conversation through the door and Stan always said it was because I had dog ears. "Really?" I whispered to Stan. He put his finger to his lips to shush me. I bit my lip as we were walking to his car. Once it was clear to talk, I let Stan have it instead of the intended, Eric. "I'm a grown ass woman. What the hell I look like? Twenty-Seven and still living at home." I yelled at him in aggravation. "She got rid of my apartment like I asked her to do that. He wants me to see a therapist. And when the hell were you going to tell me that you got drafted to the pros? I mean, I'm gone and no one writes, calls or visits, and y'all wonder why I got an attitude." I was beyond pissed at this moment. "Kait,

Kait." I could barely hear him calling my name as I kept yelling. I finally stopped talking so he could give his excuse. "First, I was going to tell you today. Second, I did try to visit but they told me you weren't allowed to have visitors. Third, I couldn't visit you because I was finishing up with school, and I was gone constantly to training camp." I couldn't be mad at him for wanting to finish school. I was proud that he did what most guys wouldn't do if they were offered a professional contact to play football.

When Stan and I arrived at the shopping strip, I couldn't help but wonder what I needed to do with my life now that I wasn't a prisoner anymore. I thought about going back to school to study counseling, but I don't think that would be wise. I got enough problems of my own that I need to take care of. So, the only other choice I had was to get a job with the family law firm considering the fact that I did finish school for that. I didn't want to do it, but I refuse to sit around in the house with them all day doing nothing.

"So, what do you wanna do first?" Stan asked me. "Well, I want to get something done to this head and then my nails and all that good stuff." I said as I was picking at my nails and scratching my head. "Yeah, 'cause today you are looking just a little bit rough like you just rolled out of bed without touching your head." He said as he tried to pick at my head. "Shut the hell up." I responded with a long eye roll.

I noticed that the town had gotten a bit crowded since I left. I really don't remember the shopping strip being this crowed in the morning. I was relieved to see that my beautician was still in the same spot because I sure didn't have time to look for someone else. "Well, you go ahead and do your girly stuff and just call me when you're ready." Stan said as I was opening the door to get out. "You trying to be funny?" I said while sitting in the car with the door propped open. "What? I don't wanna sit around in no damn salon listening to you females talk about how men are all dogs." He replied in a girly voice trying to imitate what he thinks goes on in salons. "Now how am I going to call you? No cell phone." I held my hands out as if I was holding an imaginary cell phone. "They got a phone in there that you can use." He said to me. "Kiss my ass." I told him rudely because who goes anywhere without a cell phone these days. I was gonna look like I was from the past if I asked to us their phone. "Aight, chill...chill. I'll just go get one added to my line." Stan said as he was pulling out his phone. "You'll do that for me?" I asked. "Yes, you know I would do anything for you, Kait. You like the little sister I never had and a woman I will have." He said as he was grinning and rubbing his bald head. "That was so disturbing. It's like you saying you wanna sleep with your sister." I told him as he noted that he was only joking. "By the way how are you paying for all of this?" He asked me. "Stanley, you forgot? I'm a Thomas, store credit baby." I said as I was getting out of his car.

I wasn't nervous about being out and people wondering where I've been because I'm quite sure that my "so called" parents came up with an excuse. They couldn't risk the corruption of the family name if everyone knew the truth neither could they afford what people would think if they found out where I've been the last three years. Come to think of it, I wondered how they were able to keep the doctors and nurses from snitching. Because everyone knows that when you're well-known and considered perfect, people try to find your flaw. I really didn't care how they did it honestly. I really just wanted to focus on getting my life back together.

Once I finished pampering myself, I peeped outside the door to see if I could see Stan. I told him that it would only take about three hours, but to him that's four hours. "Hey, can I use your phone?" I asked my beautician as she was getting ready for another client. "Sure, honey, and next time let me know when you're gonna be gone on charity events. You know I'm always looking for a way to boost my business." She said as she handed the phone. See, what I mean? They were able to come up with an excuse for me being gone for so long. I dialed Stan's number and he didn't answer on the first try, so I called him again. "Yo, this me." He picked up in an aggressive tone. "Is that how you answer your phone?" I asked in a high pitch voice. "Who dis?" He said smartly. "Who the hell do you think it is?" I said. "I don't know, you called me." He yelled. "Bring yo damn ass on and stop playing." I yelled back. "Oh, my bad. Aight, I'm on my way." Stan said as he now realized who I was. "Meet me at that restaurant at the corner I saw." I told him. "You talking about the Tasty Food & Bar?" He asked. "If it was at the corner, then, yes, that's the one." I quickly hung up the phone as he was talking.

I didn't wait for him to pull up in order to walk with me to the restaurant. Cassandra and Eric were already treating me like a child and I didn't need it from him, too. The breeze felt so good blowing through my new relaxed hair. I've always enjoyed spring weather because it's not too cold and it's not too hot, the temperature is just right. "Pardon me?" What now I said to myself. I slowly turned around and as the wind blew a few strands of hair on my face I swiped it away with my hand to see who was disturbing me. "Wow!" A man said as he was surprised that a black woman could have hair like this. "Excuse me.?" I said to him. "I'm sorry I don't mean to be rude or stare, but you are eye catching." He said with amazement. "What did you just say to me? Eye Candy? Listen here, that mess may work with other bitches, but this bitch right here, ain't the one. So, why don't you find someone else to play with?" I snapped as I was shaking my head and pointing my finger towards other chicks walking. "Whoa. Whoa. Whoa. No, I said catching, catching and not candy. I'm sorry it was probably my accent that threw you off." This strange man was basically apologizing for giving me a compliment. I was sort of embarrassed that I just cussed this man out for no reason. "Well, my bad. It really did sound like you said candy and not catching. You have a very strong accent?" I told this stranger who was hovering over me at about six foot, seven inches tall. "Not a problem." He said. I was waiting for him to continue, but he was just staring. "How about taking a picture. It'll last longer." I said as I stared at this tall, well-built white man. "I'm sorry. Your beauty threw me off." He said with a smile. Boy, this guy is corny as hell. "I'm looking for the courthouse actually." He replied as he was looking around. "Well, it's right around the corner if you'll just go two blocks up and you should see it." I said pointing him in the right direction. "Okay, thanks." I shook my head in a welcome gesture and started on my way when I heard his voice again. "Excuse me." I hesitantly turned around wondering what words I was gonna misunderstand this time. "I'm Keith by the way." He was extending his hand for a handshake while I had my arms crossed. He noticed that I wasn't interested in shaking hands so he slowly pulled it back hoping that I would change my mind and return the gesture. "Keith is it? Again, sorry for blowing up on you like that. You just kind of caught me off guard." I said trying not to be so rude to this strange man. "No, it's my bad I should have just asked for directions and not try to flirt." He was still smiling showing his pearly white perfect teeth. "Do you have a name or should I just call you gorgeous?" He said. "I really gotta be on my way." I said to him as I was getting tired of his corny pickup lines. "Well, gorgeous it was nice to meet you. I do hope that we run into each other again." He was holding his hand out again for a hand shake. I grabbed his hand in response to his gesture and before I knew it he lifted it up and kissed it softly with his soft pink lips. It actually felt good, but I couldn't let him know it. When he let go of my hand, I could see his shining blue eyes looking into mine. I stopped staring at his eyes and started looking at him from top to bottom without moving my head. I noticed a dimple in his chin on his well shaven

face to match his well combed brown hair. Wait, what
the hell am I saying and doing. "Oh, there's my friend
I gotta go." I told him as I saw Stan parking his car.
"Sure, it was nice meeting you again." He said with a
smile. I didn't respond as I walked by him trying to
hide the fact that he really smelled good.

"Who was that?" Stan asked as he was walking towards me. "Oh, some guy who was lost." I said shrugging my shoulders. "So when y'all going out?" He said
while he elbowing me and winking his eye. "Stan,
I am not you. I don't jump on everything with legs
that say I'm eye catching." I heard Stan laughing as
we were sitting down at a table. "Wait, wait. He said
that? Bo, that has got to be the corniest line ever." He
said as he was still chuckling a little. "Well, it's no different than saying, Stan the man." I said to him. "Hey,
don't hate the game, hate the player." I rolled my eyes
at him as he was still grinning at the fact that he was
a player. "Anyway! Listen, I've decided to work for the
law firm." I told him in order to change the subject
regarding Keith. "Say what?" He stopped looking at
the menu to ask me that question. "If working for Eric is gonna keep me sane, then that's what I gotta
do. Plus, I gotta figure out how to get this doctor to
deem me independent." I said while rubbing my forehead. "Clear you? I thought you were clear which was
why they let you come home." Stan asked with a confused look on his face. "Nope, Eric made it really clear
this morning that the doctor said that I am unsta-
ble to live by myself and until I get a clearance. I am
S.O.L!" I said holding my thumb and finger up to my
temple in reference to a gun as I pulled a fake trigger.

"Are you sure there's not nothing else you can do?" He asked me as our food was being brought to our table. "Honestly, no Stan. Because what other kind of job can I get making the money that I need in order to support myself? "I see your point. So, how's the food? I know it's better then what you were getting in the nut house." Stan asked as he was trying to make me feel better, but instead he insulted me. "You so damn insensitive." I said as I was putting food on my fork. "Kait, you are cold hearted. Nothing hurts you. Well, almost nothing." He said as he stopped eating and began staring at me. Ah, man here it comes. "Now, tell me what had you so upset yesterday?" He inquired. "Nothing, Stan just leave it alone alright." I said as I kept eating. "No, I'm not gonna leave it alone. Just like that day when you disappeared. I came to your house to see if you wanted to catch a movie and no answer. I called your cell phone, disconnected. I called your mom and she said that y'all had a big argument and hadn't seen you since. Okay, I'll buy that. But, after days go by still no answer? So, I finally go see your dad at the golf course demanding to know what was going on. He tells me that you had a nervous breakdown after taking your finals and they thought it was best that you get professional help." He was rambling on and on. I didn't wanna talk about this at least not in a public place. Stan was hitting all of the right buttons. I was getting emotional because he was my best friend and we never ever kept secrets from each other. No matter if it was good or bad we shared everything. I fought back the tears as I told him this wasn't the place to talk about my personal business. He calmed down and apologized. I told him that it was okay and that I appreciated his concern. Stan didn't need to know the truth. I know they say that the truth will set you free, but in my case the truth would do the opposite.

CHAPTER 3

Damn, I look good. I thought to myself. Although I was glad I was going to be making some money, I still wasn't pleased with the fact that I had to work for this damn man. Well, technically he's retired and doesn't trust Cassandra with the firm, plus she don't know a thing about running a company. So, that leaves me to run it. Eric may not like me and probably doesn't trust me either, but I was able to make partner with a law firm before taking my bar. Now that is something you don't see every day and Eric was impressed with the fact that I was always top in my class and won all my cases during internship.

I was checked my makeup in the mirror by the door before I left and yelled to them I was leaving. "Wait a second." Eric yelled back. I stood at the door with my hand on my hip wondering what the hell he wanted. "I know that you probably called Stanley to pick you up to take you to work, but that just wouldn't look professional. Don't you agree?" He was handing me some car keys at this point. Ugh, I hated the fact that he bought me a car because it will felt like he was doing me a favor. Bad enough, I'm the HNIC at the law firm and now this. "You didn't have to do that." I said as I opened my hand so that he could drop the keys in them. As I was walking to the black Lexus I could see Stan pulling up. "I thought you needed me to take you to work." He yelled out his window. "I did too." I said as I opened my door. "Woo. Hot mama! You got a date with ol' boy later?" I knew he was referring to Keith. "Look, you ass. Unlike you I have to actually do some work in order to get paid." I said while rubbing my hands together to suggest I was talking about money. "What? Football is work. You think that it's easy running up and down the field in the rain, sleet, snow?" He said as he was pointing to the palm of his hand. "Do it look like I care?" I said as I was getting in my car. "Kait?" Stan said with a concerned tone in his voice. I didn't say anything. I just stood there waiting for him to say another smart comment. "Please, behave, and if you need to talk......" I didn't let him finish his sentence. I just simply rolled my eyes, gave him the bird, and got in the car.

While I was walking up the stairs to the courthouse I could feel eyes watching me in amazement. The guys wanted me and the women hated me. Everyone knew who I was automatically. Another bad thing about being well known in a small town is that everyone knows everybody's business. Well, almost everybody's business. They can't know too much about our personal business if my beautician thinks that I've been traveling all over the states doing charity work. Please, who would believe that foolishness? Anyway it felt good to be envied. Even though this wasn't my choice of work, I knew that in the end it would pay off after a while.

When I entered the building, I noticed a scent that seemed familiar to my nose. I knew I smelled it before but I just wasn't sure where. I ignored my nose for a minute while I tried to find out where my office was going to be. Then it suddenly hit me where the origin of that smell came from when I saw Keith standing in front of the elevators. He didn't see me just yet so the question remained if I should make my presence known. Hell yeah I should! If he thought I looked good in some sweat pants and a t-shirt, wait till he sees me now. "Excuse me?" I happily returned the favor and interrupted him just like he interrupted me the other day. As he turned around, I noticed he licked his lips in pleasure before speaking. "Once again you are eye catching. I said catching, okay. Not candy." I chuckled a little because I remembered how our first conversation went. "Well, thank you. So, what are you doing here? Did you not come here the other day? Never mind. It's none of my business." I said waving my hand in the air to dismiss my question. "No, I'm actually....." He stopped as a woman came over and interjected. "Ms. Thomas, I'm here to show you to your office." The woman said to me. "Okay, I'll meet you down the hall in a minute." I told her as she shook her head in agreement and walked towards the end of the hall. "Now, what where you saying?" I asked Keith. "Ms. Thomas? As in the Thomas Law Firm? As in the Thomas County Courthouse?" He said with a surprised look on his face. "Yes, but I'm only adopted into the family name and business. All this stuff belongs to my adoptive parents." I could tell that once Keith found out who I was that he became nervous as he played with his gold watch. We had been standing in front of the elevators letting it go up and down as neither one of us was ready to go our separate ways. I was feeling bold that day so I said the first thing that came to my mind. "So, you said you hope we would see each other again, right?" I asked in a very flirtatious way. "Yes." He responded with a smile. Damn, he has a sexy smile. "So, what now?" I asked him. "Well, that's entirely up to you. I can give you my number and you can do whatever you please with it." He said as he was holding out his hands and shrugging his shoulders letting me know that he was giving me the upper hand. I rather you do with me however you please. I was said in my head as his scent was making me hot. "Okay, I'll go out on a limb here and take your number." I said slowly making sure not to say what I was thinking at the time. He shook his head and smiled as he was waiting for me to put it in my phone. I could see the lady pointing to her watch as I finished programing his number. "I hate to rush off, but I really gotta go. It was nice seeing you again." I said as I was walking past him. "You too. Have a good day." He said as I knew he was watching me strut down the hallway. "Thanks." I replied not wanting to turn around because I already knew he was staring me down.

Everyone felt my presence as we entered the suite full of lawyers and clerks. I knew right away that the office down the hall was mine considering that it was the biggest one from the others. Before the clerk left,

I informed her that I wanted a meeting with all the lawyers in fifteen minutes. She gave me a look like how was she supposed to do that. I waited for her to say something smart as I didn't have a problem with telling her ass off. I wanted to make sure that everyone was doing their job because I didn't have time for mistakes. Plus if nothing is done right, then Eric will bring his ass down here and I would just rather not go there with him.

I stood in the board room looking at the clock. It has been over fifteen minutes and not one person was in there. So, if they didn't want to come to me then I would go to them. But, before I could even reach the doorknob it was opening. "Finally, I think I've waited long enough." I said as I walked to the head of the office table. "Wow, I wasn't expecting that." A man voice said. I felt my pressure go up and my blood boil when I looked up and saw my ex fiancé walking in. "Ms. Thomas I'm so sorry. I tried to stop him but he insisted...." I interrupted. "What is your name?" I asked her. "Carmen." She replied. "Well, Carmen please let everyone know that the meeting will start within the next ten minutes and close the door behind you." I told her.

"What are you doing here, Zavier?" I asked furiously. "Didn't Eric tell you that I was coming by? I just got back in town from a doctor's convention and when I heard you were back, I had to come see you." He said extending his arms out expecting a hug. "You still didn't answer my question. Why are you here? I don't want you here. I didn't ask for you. I don't want to ...." He grabbed and kissed me to keep me from mouthing another word. I pushed him away with force that I didn't know I had. "I see you still don't know how to stop talking." He boasted proudly like he actually just did something. "Zavier, I want you to leave. Now!" I hurriedly showed him to the door. He took a minute walking to it, but he eventually got the picture. I moved back scared he would do it again. "I'll be seeing you soon, love." He said while stroking my chin. I slammed the door behind him. I like his nerve to pop back in here like he owns me. I sure hope he don't think that we are just going to pick up where we left off. It was his lost and not mine. My thoughts were running together I was so angry. Ugh, I don't think I can afford any more disappointments or surprises today. I picked up the phone and called Stan. "Hey, when I get off we need to go get a drink." I said while rubbing my forehead as it felt like another headache was coming on. "It's been one of those days already?" He chuckled. "You have no idea." I told him. "Cool, meet me on Tone Boulevard. There is a new club called The Vibe that just opened." I agreed to meet Stan there to relieve some of this tension. The only thing now is to make it through the rest of the day without cracking.

I had one drink in my hand and another one in the other. "Hey, I think you should slow down some." Stan said as he tried to take a drink from me. "No, I need this. Besides, you were always the one who couldn't hold their liquor." I reminded him as I took two shots of Tequila to the head and ordered two more. This was just what I needed to ease my mind from the awful day I had. For some reason, I had a feeling that matters were going to get worse and not better at work. No one liked the thought of a young black woman being the boss. I thought about letting up a bit. But then they would think that I am weak and take it for granted. I needed to stop stressing over that job and enjoy my night. "Aww...that's my jam." I said while throwing my hand up in the air. The DJ started to play some Reggae. I don't know what it was about Reggae, but when it played, you couldn't help but move. I grabbed Stan to come dance with me before the song ended, but he shook his head no. He told me to go ahead and that he would watch my drink while I danced. I threw the last two shots of Tequila back and gave him the empty glasses. He laughed as I patted my chest to try to relieve the burning sensation. I started putting my hands on my thick hips as I was dirty whining my ass in a seductive way. The song was getting into my body even more as I put my hands on my knees to get low. While I was enjoying myself, I felt hands on my flat stomach which pulled me back. I knew this wasn't nobody but Stan. I didn't turn around to check and see if it was him. I just grinded even more sexual to let him know he couldn't keep up. The hands was holding me tighter as they were keeping up with my hips moving around and around, from side to side. I raised up from the bent position to congratulate him for keeping up with me, but I was very surprised when I turned around to see that it wasn't Stan. "Keith?" I said with a confused look. "Gorgeous, Kaitlyn?" He tried to act like he was as surprised as I was when I realized that it was him, but I could tell that he wasn't. "Sorry, I thought you were my friend." I apologized to him. "Well, as you can see I'm not." He said smiling. "What? I didn't tell you my name, did I?" I quizzed him when I realized what he said "Well, no, you didn't Ms. Thomas, and you know what when I asked people for your name, they had a fear in their eyes. What did you do in order for them to fear you?" Keith asked as we were walking back to the bar. "It's not me they fear, it's the last name. Let's just say that you don't mess with Eric Thomas and I'll leave it at that. But, I'm nothing like them." I told him. "Are you sure? I mean our first encounter was pretty intense. I thought you were gonna jump me?" He said putting his hands up as if were under arrest. "Fuc....." I paused as I had to catch myself before using the F bomb. "Whatever!" I said in correction. "Nope, that's not what you really wanted to say." He said as we both laughed. We continued our conversation as I started looking for Stan. I was pretty sure that he was probably in a corner somewhere with a chick. "Can I buy you a drink?" He asked as I was still looking for Stan. "No, it's getting late and I have to go to work in the morning." I told him as I hopped down from the bar stool. "Looking for your boyfriend?" Keith wondered as he noticed that during our entire conversation my eyes where elsewhere. "No, my friend." I said to correct him. "C'mon, really? You gonna use the "friend" thing?" He said as he looked me up and down as I did to him the other day. "Like I said friend, and what do you mean by that anyway?" I questioned as I folded my arms. "Nothing, I'm just saying that there is no way that a woman as gorgeous as you is single.

You can't be single and if you are single then there are two reason why. One, you're crazy, or two you're a lesbian." He said in a very matter fact tone before he took a sip of his scotch. I ordered two more shots before speaking to Keith because as bad as I wanted to curse him out, I couldn't. Instead I laughed and told him the reason why I was single. "Well one I am crazy, and two, I am not a lesbian, and three, I was engaged, but that's something I rather not discuss with a complete stranger." I told him as I made a bee-line towards the door. "We can fix that right now. I'm Keith Palmerson and I have my own traveling agency. I like long walks on the beach and I like to listen to reggae music. Some people say I look like Channing Tatum, but I think I look better. Your turn." He said to me as he ordered more drinks. I laughed a little as I was listening to him trying to narrate himself in ten seconds. I was kind of impressed by the way he described himself in the minimum time he had. "Well, that's all nice, but I see my friend." I said while pointing to the exit. "Ah, man that's not fair." He pouted as he turned around to look at Stan. "I tell you what, if we ever run into each other again, we can finish our conversation." I told him as we hugged. I didn't know this man, but yet I let him hug me. I knew then that I was drunk off my ass.

Stan told me that he needed to take me home AS-AP. I asked him why and he said that Eric was looking for me. "I don't need him looking for me. I am grown and he is not my real dad. Who does he think he is? He better run Cassandra like that because he sure in hell don't run nothing over here." Stan was holding

my arm while I was fussing to keep me from falling.
"It would have been a lot worse if he would have actually came in." Stan said as he opened the door for
me. "Wait, wait. You mean to tell me that he was actually here? But, how did he..? I paused and remembered that Zavier came back by and asked what I was
doing later. So, like an idiot I told him, but it was only to make him jealous. "I need to stay over tonight. I
can't go home like this unless you're prepared to bail
me out of jail." I demanded of Stan as he started the
car. He immediately picked up his phone to inform
Eric of where I was gonna be. I couldn't believe that
this man actually came down to the club looking for
me. "He said that it would be best if you didn't and he
said that you better be at work tomorrow too." Stan
relayed his message word for word. I rolled my eyes
and held up my middle finger since I wasn't able to
speak because I had opened the door to throw up.
"Aye, man, you better not throw up in my car and I'm
not carrying your ass either." Stan scolded me as he
waited for me to finish. I remained silent after closing
Stan's car door because talking was starting to make
my head hurt. Besides, I was still trying to enjoy my
night enough I couldn't hold my liquor.

CHAPTER 4

The morning had set in and I wasn't feeling my best. I pushed myself to get to up and get ready for work because I refused to lose this war to Eric. He's already won so many battles and it was time for that to stop. "Hey, I laid your bag by the dresser." Stan said as knocked to let his presence be known. "Thanks." I told him. I was glad to have a friend like Stan because he took care of me last night, plus he went over to Eric's to grab me some clean clothes. It's true that we both sometimes can get on each other nerves, but if one of us is in need, we will always be there no matter what.

I went into the kitchen to get me a big cup of coffee to help with this hangover, but instead my hangover got worst. "What the hell were you thinking last night? You are representing me and it was very irresponsible for you to be getting drunk." Eric yelled. "Why are they here?" I asked Stan as I saw Cassandra in the hallway. "Kait, they're just checking on you to make sure that you are okay? You were drinking pretty heavy last night and you can't mix alcohol with medication." He said as he tried to touch my shoulder. "I don't have time for this." I told them as I moved before Stan could touch my shoulder. "I need you to move so I can get to work." I shouted at Eric. "I'm not done talking and you need to realize that your actions reflect us. I want you to get it together. Do you understand me?" I was ignoring him the whole entire time. "Eric, stop it. She just went out. There's nothing wrong with that." Cassandra said as she placed her hand on his back to get him to calm down. "I don't think that I was talking to you." Eric said to her as he moved so she couldn't touch his back. "Kaitlyn, you're an adult and the boss at my law firm. I mean it. I'm not playing with you anymore." Eric said as he was pointing his finger at me. "Glad those days are over...." I said before slamming the door. "What did she mean by that, Eric?" Cassandra asked looking confused. "Nothing babe, I'm sorry I yelled at you. It's just that I care so much about her even though she not my flesh and blood. I just want her to know that everything we do is for her own good." Eric said as he was holding Cassandra to get her mind off the last thing that was said. "Thanks for watching her, but I gotta say Stan, you aren't making smart choices yourself." Eric sternly voiced his opinion to Stan. "Well, with all due respect, sir, she is a grown woman and she is capable of making her own decisions." Stan told him as they walked out of the door. "I'm sorry Stan, forgive my husband. He just don't know how to express his feelings." Cassandra stated as she hugged Stan goodbye.

While I was still trying to get over this hangover, I asked Carmen to go through my schedule for today. She informed me that I had a meeting with a client in an hour. Yes, finally some action. "Okay, I need the entire file copied. I want the originals to everything and place the copied documents in their file." I instructed her. "Yes, Ms. Thomas." She said as she took the files off my desk and exited out of my office. I looked down at my desk to start preparing when I noticed a sealed envelope on my desk with my name on it. Who the hell been in my office without my permission? I sat down to read the contents of the letter. I was pretty sure it was from Zavier; However, I was wrong. The letter stated:

Dear Kait,

I enjoyed our time last night as well as our conversation (wink). The reason for this letter is because you have yet to use my phone number, so I went old fashion and decided to write you. I do hope that I can officially take you out on a date where there is less noise and more decent meals. If you still have my number, feel free to use it any time of day. No matter the hour.

Sincerely Yours,

Keith Palmerson

I immediately smiled as I finished reading the letter. That really made my day because I actually enjoyed Keith's company yesterday. The only thing to do now is to give him a call and maybe think about going out on a date with him. I closed my eyes for a minute thinking about Keith and what he looks like without any clothes on. "Excuse me, Ms. Thomas your 9:30 is here." I looked at the clock on my computer assuming that it was correct with the time of 8:30 showing. "They're an hour early." I told her. "Yes,

I told him that you were busy, but." I held my hand up as I just wanted Carmen to stop talking. I asked her if she had the paperwork finished she hesitated to respond. I walked pass this short, light skin of a woman who apparently didn't know how to do her job. I entered the conference room without even knocking first. I didn't care at this point. I just wanted to know who this person is who thinks that they can just do whatever they feel. When I entered, I saw Zavier standing in front of the window looking down at the street. "Man, this is a lovely view." He announced. I closed the door and asked him what he was doing here. I informed him that I had a meeting. He shook his head and said that he knew that. "Then, why the hell are you still standing here? Leave!" I basically tried not to scream at him. "Now, yesterday it seemed like you didn't have any time to talk. So I figured that if I made an appointment, then you would have to talk to me." He said while motioning for me to sit down with him. "I don't have time for these games, okay. This is my job. I am at work. If you wanna play, I suggest you go find that bitch who had your attention." I said as I refused to sit down with him. He was walking over to comfort me as he saw the pain in my eyes when I reminded him of his infidelity. "Kait, I'm sorry. I shouldn't have cheated on you. It was wrong. I don't have any excuses for what I did, but I'm regretting it every day that I don't get to wake up next to you." He was being very apologetic while holding my hands. I wasn't sure if it was the conversation with Eric this morning or if it was what Zavier was saying, but a tear forced it way out of my right eye. He gently wiped it with is thumb and pulled me close. "You don't understand how bad you hurt me. You knew that I had issues with trust and yet you did that to me. How could you do that? We were supposed to be married. We were supposed to be happy. I was supposed to be your one and only. You were supposed to be my first. How...." Before I could ask him the question again, he was kissing me. Only this time I welcomed it and returned the favor by massaging his tongue with mine. I felt Zavier hands caressing me slowly on my ass as he grabbed it with one of his hands. Meanwhile, I was rubbing his wavy jet black hair, not wanting him to stop. This passion of heat was interrupted with a knock at the door. "Just a minute." I said as we were both getting ourselves together. "Come in." I called out. "Ms. Thomas, Judge Henderson is requesting the presence of a lawyer ASAP." Carmen said as she peeked her head in. "Okay, send Victor over." I said as I rubbed my lips together. "Well, Victor was the one who was dismissed from the case because he knew the defendant." She said as she was now completely in the meeting room. "Tell them I'll be right over." I waited for her to close the door before asking him what just happened. He leaned in trying to finish what we started. I pushed him back and told him that this was too much. "We'll talk about this later." I told him as I moved my hands in a circle motion letting him know that I was referring to what just happened. "Sure, um, you want me to call you or come by?" He probed. "I'll call you later. Is your number still the same?" I replied back. "Oh, no I changed it." He was shaking his head no. "Well, just leave your number with Carmen and I'll give you a call later." I said as I left Zavier in the meeting room. Carmen waited for Kaitlyn to leave before going in the meeting room with Zavier. "What the hell was that?" Carmen asked Zavier. "Shh…….Close the door." He whispered as he pulled her in hoping no one saw her. "You knew that we were supposed to be married so don't even go there." Zavier answered Carmen as she bit her lips in frustration. "Yes, but do you have to be all in her face like that?" She sneered. "If this is going to work, I have to play Mr. Nice guy, okay. And, if that means kissing her, babying her, or sleeping with her, then that's what I'm going to do." He professed while comforting Carmen. "Like hell, if you even think about sleeping with her I'm going to tell her everything." Zavier grabbed his face before putting Carmen into an aggressive choke hold. "Bitch, if you mess this up, I promise you that it will be the last thing you do." He told her as he had her pinned up against the wall with is hand around her throat. "You hurting me, let go." She murmured with fear in her watery eyes. "Now, listen give her my number and don't say a word about this. Understand?" He told her as he shook her neck with his hand still around it letting her know that he meant business. She was silent. "I can't hear you." He shook it again. "Yes." She whimpered. "That's a good girl, now give daddy some sugar and do what I asked." He slowly released her from his grip.

    I was proud of myself in the courtroom today, you couldn't tell that I was just released from the mental institution with the way I handled that case. "Carmen, I'm going to lunch. So forward the important calls to my cell phone and send all appointment calls to my office phone. I'll check it when I get back." I told her as I was headed out to meet with Stan. "Yes, Ms. Thomas." I think that she was finally getting the picture. "Did Mr. Price leave a number where he could be reached?" I asked. "Yes, it's right here. I hope I'm not out of line, but it looks like you two have a history." I snatched the paper out of her hand. "You're right. You are out of line." I scowled before answering my cell phone. "Yo, where you at." Stan requested my whereabouts. "I work around the corner. You acting like it's gonna take me a long time to get there." I told him as I was getting on the elevator. "Well, hurry yo ass up." I hung up the phone in his face again. He was starting to get worrisome now.

I laughed a little as I passed by my beautician's beauty shop because that was the same spot where I snapped on Keith. "I'm here." I said to Stan while entering the restaurant. "Yeah, I can see that now." He said as he was drinking a beer. "So, is today any better?" He asked. "If seeing Zavier today was considered any better then, no." I answered back. "Zavier? When did you see him?" Stan was looking concerned now? I told him that he came by the office yet again and I didn't want to talk about him. "Can we have a nice lunch, please?" I pleaded with Stan as I was motioning for the waitress. "Sure. But, you know I wanna know what was happening between you and that white dude." Stan insinuated. "Nothing. We were just dancing." I said as I had finished placing my order with the waitress. Stan was going on and on about how me and Keith were dancing with each other. I wanted him to shut the hell up talking about it because he was getting on my nerves. "Will you just finish ordering your damn food?" I said to him as the waitress was just standing there tapping her pin on her pad. "So, what's Vanilla Ice's name?" Stan wondered with a questionable look on his face. I forgot that I didn't mention his name to Stan. "His name is Keith." I said staring out the window. "So, like you into white guys now?" He asked curiously as if me and Keith were dating. "Look, I gotta be back in court in three hours, so please, can we just eat?" I informed Stan as the waitress arrived with our food. "Can I get you anything else, sir?" The waitress said as she winked and licked her lips at Stan. "No, sweetie I'm good. Thanks." Stan blushed. I noticed she was still standing there, so I asked for an extra sauce for my steak. "Oh, no this heffa didn't." I exclaimed as she completely ignored me and left our table. Stan thought that it was hilarious, but I didn't find it funny at all. "Told you that no one can resist Stan the man." He said as he rubbed his chest at the table. I rolled my eyes and advised him to get over himself because in case he hadn't noticed, the women that he attracted didn't have nothing more than a high school education and that can only get you so far.

As we were finishing our lunch I could tell that Stan had something on his mind. "Okay, what is it?" I asked Stan as he was just staring at me and rubbing his chin. "Nothing, I'm just trying to figure out why we never dated." He replied. "Well when we met Stan, I was only twelve so I don't think that I knew much about relationships." I told him as I took a sip of my water. "You know what I mean, smart ass. I'm talking about in high school and after that." He sarcastically responded as he sat up from his chair. I was trying to figure out in the nicest way to tell Stan that he was a hoe because all I could remember was him with a different girl every time I saw him. "Stan, you were never with the same girl for more than a week. So, why would I put myself in that position?" I asked him as I was getting my things together. "You're right, but don't you know that maybe you could have been the woman to change me?" He questioned as he held his heart. "Stan, a woman shouldn't have to do that. You should want to change for yourself. I gotta go because I see that waitress is eager for me to leave so she can come and serve herself to you." I gave him the peace sign to let him know I was about to leave. I had thought about dating Stan at one time, but we had gotten so close that I thought that it might have just been weird. We were the best of friends and because I considered him like a brother, I just couldn't see him as more.

Stan kept motioning for me to sit down as I kept telling him that I had to go. "What now boy?" I was annoyed by this time with him that I plopped down with all my stuff. "Talk to me." Stan stated. I looked at him like he was crazy trying to figure out what in the hell he was talking about. "I thought that I was since we've been here?" I replied back to him with a confused look. "No, I mean tell me about the other night and why were you so upset?" He asked. Stan was always the type of person who never let things go. Even if he saw how uncomfortable it made you, he still wanted to know because he felt like talking always made things better. "Stan, like I told you then it was nothing just leave it alone." I stated. I could tell that he was getting annoyed with my answers, but I refused to tell him the truth because I knew that he wouldn't look at me the same. "Alright, but you can't keep holding that stuff in because what's gonna happen is that it's all gonna come out in one big explosion and you're not gonna know how to handle it." He informed me. "What are you my psychologist?" I asked since he seemed to know it all. "No, smart ass I'm just telling you what I know." He mumbled as he was getting up to walk me out. I asked him if he was gonna wait to get the waitress number and he said that she wasn't his type. "Don't put up your player card because I'm here." I laughed. Stan didn't think it was funny as he shot me the bird and told me to get back to work before Eric fired my ass. I loved Stan with everything in me, but there was just certain things that he didn't need to know.

CHAPTER 5

I stayed at the office late that night because I wanted to be sure that my case for the morning was prepared, but in truth I was full of confusion and I just didn't feel like dealing with Eric when I got home. I kept thinking about how I was hiding my secret from Stan and how I and Zavier kissed. Most of my mind was on Eric and there were no good thoughts coming to mind. All I could think about was how he is acting like everything is good between us when it's not. He is so full of himself right now thinking that he has control over me, but he doesn't. I felt my eyes starting to water up as I went to thinking about all the pain that I've endured over the years since I've been adopted by that bastard. I wanted to call Stan for comfort, but I knew he would make a big fuss about it and I didn't want to prove him right by not talking to him earlier. Zavier was the last person that I needed to talk too considering I knew what was on his agenda.

Instead, I sucked all the tears up and tried focusing on my work. I was able to do that for a while until I came across Keith's letter. I read it again to see if I could read in between the lines and find a hidden message. I couldn't find a hidden message. He was just pretty much straight forward. I looked over at the clock on my desk to see what time it was. It was a little after ten. I remembered he said to call him no matter the time. I picked up the office phone because I didn't want him to have my cell phone number yet. "Hello?" Keith said in a sleepy voice. I wanted to hang up. "Sorry, I didn't mean to call so late." I said trying to clear my voice hoping he wouldn't notice that I've been crying. "No, Kait its fine. But, what's wrong?" I heard the genuine concern in his voice. I'm thinking damn maybe I shouldn't have called, or maybe a part of me wanted him to know that something was wrong. Why? I don't know. I mean, I barely knew this man and yet when I am around him, I feel so comfortable. "How did you know that something was wrong?" I asked still trying to clear my voice. "Kait, where are you?" He asked again with a sincere tone. "Well, I'm still at the office working late. I have a big case in the morning. So everything has to be perfect. I can't make no mistakes or it'll be my ass handed to me by Eric." For some reason I started crying again. I tried to stop but I couldn't. "Kait, Kait. I'm coming over there, okay?" I heard Keith demands loud and clear despite my deep sobbing. "Keith, that's unnecessary. I'll be okay." I told him as I tried to get myself together. He told me that he lived fifteen minutes away but he could get there in five. I assured him that I would be fine and definitely appreciated his concerns. It felt nice to know that he cared enough to get out of his bed to make sure I was okay.

Before, I could start my car I noticed I had left my cell phone. I wasn't gonna go back and get it, but Keith made me promised to call him when I got in the car since I wouldn't let him come to the office. As I opened the car door, I dropped my keys on the ground and was trying to pick them up with my pinky finger. That's how tired I was. It wasn't going so well, so I decided to get out to pick them up, but on my way back up I saw the light reflect a masked shadow in my driver window. I opened my mouth to scream, but he covered it with his gloved hand. I bit his finger as hard as I could as he was trying to lift me. I was kicking up against my car hoping that someone would hear the noise. I was so exhausted from working hard that day that my body became easy for him to drag. I was praying in my head, praying that he wouldn't kill me. The only person I could think about was Stan. If I was going to die, I didn't wanna leave without telling him the truth. During my struggles with this masked stranger, he held a knife to my throat. I stopped fighting because I knew he was serious about killing me. I didn't know what this man wanted, or if he even he had the right person. I just wanted him to stop and let me go. "Hey! Hey!" I heard a voice yell from afar. The headlights were blinding me so I couldn't see who it was. The man wasn't scared as he held on tight to me while dragging my shoeless feet. The man who came to my rescue charged in our direction with such force that the man finally let me go. I fell to the grass feeling scared to death about what just happened. "Are you okay?" Keith examined me while looking around simultaneously making sure that the man was gone. I grabbed onto his neck without responding. He was holding me so tight, his body language wanted to make sure I was alright. I shook my head no because I was still holding on and crying hysterically. He scooped me up and mentioned I needed to go to the hospital. I didn't wanna go, but because Keith saved my life, I readily obliged.

"Well, it looks like you're gonna be fine." The doctor told me. "The police are on their way to ask you a few questions. Are you okay with that?" I shook my head slowly up and down to let him that I was okay to answer some questions. "I'm glad I didn't listen to you and followed my first mind." Keith said. "It wasn't necessary." I replied. "You're stubborn, you know that?" He reminded me as he leaned back in the hospital chair. "So, I've been told." I answered back groggily as I closed my eyes from the shot they gave me earlier to get me to calm down. "What the hell is going here?" Eric yelled as he walked in. Why was his ass here? I didn't call him nor did I tell any of the nurses to call him. But like I said before, they don't want nobody to know their business and I'm pretty sure that he has a spy up here. "How you doing sir? I'm Keith. I brought..." Keith said as he was introducing himself to Eric. "I don't give a damn who you are, son. You need to leave!" Eric announced while moving out of the way so Keith could exit. "I asked him to stay and I don't remember calling you. So you can leave." I spoke up for Keith as I was trying to keep my eyes open because I was still drowsy from that shot. "Kaitlyn, I've had enough of your foolishness.

I'm sending you back first thing in the morning." Eric said. "Well, good I never wanted to leave anyway. I'd rather be there then here with you and that bitch." I finally had enough strength to my voice as I loudly disclosed this information to him. He was shocked and asked if I had lost my damn mind. Apparently I did because I wasn't thinking before I spoke. Keith was still standing in the room. He wasn't sure what we were talking about, but he knew it was something that he shouldn't be listening to. "Everyone calm down. Calm down." Zavier's voice escalated even before he entered the room. He looked upset as he saw Keith standing in the room because he wasn't sure who Keith was and why he was here with me. "Can I help you?" Zavier looked Keith up and down as he grabbed my hand to let Keith know to not even think about getting with me. "I was just leaving. Kait, call me tomorrow when you're feeling a little better." Keith said before leaving the room. "Okay, and thanks again for everything." I stated. Keith was gone and I didn't want him to leave. I rather have him here then these two pricks. "Who was that?" Zavier asked. "I don't know they gave me some kind of shot that makes me sleepy and loopy." I responded sarcastically. "I apologize, Mr. Thomas. I meant to speak to you earlier but when I heard that my baby was here, I dropped everything and focused on getting here and making sure that she was alright." Zavier said to Eric as he was walking over to shake his hand. "Why did you need to talk to Eric?" I asked Zavier with a confused expression. "No problem, Zavier. I understand. Now we need to be discreet about this. Tell me how did you find out that she was here? Because that person is gonna get fired." Eric demanded this answer from Zavier as he changed the topic. "No need, Mr. Thomas. I've already taken care of all that for you." Zavier said as he waved his hand in a cleaning motion and totally avoiding the question. "I'm gonna see if your doctor is ready to discharge you." Zavier said as he kissed me on my forehead before leaving. Eric left out with him. I knew that he only left to make sure that no one started rumors of what they think happened. I didn't care, I was just glad that they were both gone. Stan had popped in my mind again. I was going to make sure that I called him as soon as this damn shot wore off.

"Listen, you can't be talking like that in front of her!" Eric said furiously to Zavier. "I apologize, Mr. Thomas, it won't happen again. Now, are you sure that this is going to work?" Zavier asked Eric. "Hell, if this doesn't get her attention then I got something else planned for that little bitch. She thinks that I don't know that she's being trying to get cleared by the doctor. I'm gonna go ahead and let him clear her." Eric said as he was looked around making sure Kaitlyn wasn't around to hear. "Are you sure that she needs to be by herself?" Zavier asked with a concerned look. "Listen that is where you come in. I don't care what you have to do to get this done, but we don't have much time. I think Cassandra is getting suspicious, but I can handle her." Eric told Zavier as he shook his hand and instructed him to take Kaitlyn home with him.

As I laid in the guest bed at Stan's house, I couldn't help but wonder what would have happened if Keith hadn't showed up? I didn't wanna think about the possibility of what would have happened as it was causing me to cry. I heard a soft knock at the door. "Hey, you been up all night?" I shook my head yes as Stan opened the door. "Now, you know you gonna get me in some serious trouble. Did you see how Zavier was giving me the evil eye?" Stan asked as he was walking into the guest bedroom. "I wasn't gonna go home with Zavier knowing what his intentions where gonna be." I stated as I sat up in the bed. "Zavier was getting on my nerves and Eric showed up giving me all types of hell. I just didn't wanna be there anymore, okay. I just wanted to be left alone. I just wanted to feel safe again. I only...." I begin to cry hysterically. Stan was holding me tight and trying to get me to calm down. I could feel the beating of his heart against my face as I was using his chest as comfort. "Listen, I'm here. You're safe. No one is gonna hurt you, okay?" My phone started to buzz on the night stand and I knew it was probably Eric. I didn't feel like hearing his mouth right now. I asked Stan if he could answer it. He looked at me like I was talking to someone else. I laid back in the bed trying to keep my composure and thinking of other things to get my mind off of last night.

Stan finally answered the phone, but later passed it to me. I shook my head in a no gesture because I refused to hear Eric say that it was my fault about what happened last night. "Get the phone." He said to me as I was still saying no. He threw the phone on the bed and told me to get it. I gave him the bird and I got it back in return. "Yes!" I yelled into the phone. "Sorry, did I catch you at a bad time?" The voice replied. Oops, I was wrong it was my hero, Keith. "No, no I was just getting up. I really need to get ready for work." I told him. "Work? Do you know what time it is?" Keith questioned. I looked over at the clock on the nightstand and it read noon. "Oh, damn I'm late." I hurriedly jumped out of Stan's guest bed. "YOU'RE NOT GOING NO WHERE, SO SIT YO ASS DOWN!" Stan was screaming to me from the hall as if he was eaves dropping on my conversation. "Your dad?" Keith asked me. "Um, no my friend. The guy who I was at the club with the other night." I replied. "Oh, your MIA friend." He made me laugh when he reminded me of our night together. I then asked Keith how he got my number and apparently he said that I texted him around two in the morning telling him that I saw a rainbow. "I apologize, but because of my illness they gave me another shot to make sure that I remained calm and it had me high as a kite." Before I knew it I was speaking without thinking. "Well, are you okay?" Keith asked again. I told him that I was fine and I was guessing that he didn't catch on to what I said earlier which was a good thing. "Listen, may I ask you a question? And you can choose whether to answer it or not." He stated as he paused before asking me the question. "Sure." I told him as I didn't mind answering any of his questions because he did indeed saved my life. "Are you and that guy a couple? Because if looks could kill I would probably be dead right now." He asked in an uncertain tone. I remembered our unfinished conversation at the club and was debating on whether to tell Keith the reason as to why I am single. I figured that I could leave out all of the major details and just make it short and sweet. "Well, let's just say that a man doesn't know when he has a good thing until it's gone." I told Keith as I exhaled. He responded that he understood and it was the other way around for him. "I use to be married, but my wife hated that I worked so much, but I was working so that she wouldn't have to. She wanted a lavish lifestyle and I was working to make sure she had it." He later revealed that he questioned his divorce. "So, do you miss her?" I asked without even thinking. "Ugh, her laugh and smile, but the cheating, no." He chuckled after reminiscing. I think that was his way of getting me to laugh. Well, that makes two things me and Keith have in common. We both like reggae and we've both been cheated on. My heart went out to Keith as he told me the story of his ex-wife. I personally understood what it felt like to love someone so dearly and have them betray your trust. "So, he cheated on you?" Keith asked. "Huh? I didn't say that." I said as Keith kept probing. "No, you didn't say it, but you kept saying you know how it feels and that you understood. So, I'm guessing that he cheated on you." Keith stated as it was obvious that he was listening to my every word. I asked him if we could change the subject and that was when he asked if he could see me today. I told him that I didn't mind seeing him. We agreed to have lunch considering the time. I had finally forgotten about my painful night as I was trying to get ready for my date, but that was until I looked in the mirror and saw the bruise that was left from my tragic night.

CHAPTER 6

As I was getting dressed all I could think about was getting the courage to talk to Stan. I was glad to be alive, but I couldn't help but to think if Stan would ever forgive me for not telling him my secrets. "So, you and Keith?" He looked at me with a smile while I was fixing my hair. "There's nothing going on. We are just friends." I responded while trying to hide the fact that I really enjoyed talking to Keith. "Do you know how many times I've heard that?" He said. "I can only imagine." I told him as we were walking downstairs. He then asked me if I wanted to go home. I asked if he was tired of me already and he assured me he wasn't. I did need to get me some clothes, but I wasn't thrilled about sitting down with Cassandra and Eric and talking about last night. Well, at least with her anyway. He could care less about what goes on with me. Stan's phone started ringing upstairs, interrupting our conversation. He jumped up to answer it while I sat at the end of the table reading the comics section of the daily newspaper. I couldn't hear what he was saying through the walls of his three story house. I do have to say that he's being paid quite well for just training. "Now, if you gotta go.

Go ahead, I'll be fine." I told him as he entered back into the kitchen. He sighed a little. "What's wrong?" I asked. "I do have to leave." He said. "Okay? Well, go ahead I can deal with Cassandra and Eric. I'll see you later." He grabbed my hand and asked me to sit down on the couch with him. "You acting like someone just died?" I was confused as he had this serious expression on his face. "No one died." He said as he shook his head from side to side. I could understand how he was feeling when I wouldn't tell him my secret as he was prolonging to tell me what was going on with him. "Will you just say it already?" I said with frustration as he kept pausing every time he said a word. "You know I love you right." He said to me while starting me straight in my eyes. I was confused and wasn't sure where he was going with this conversation. "Okay? I love you too, Stan." I responded softly to him. "I just want you to know that what I did was out of love." Stan stammered as he was trying to find the words in order to tell Kait what he found out about Zavier. He hired a private investigator to insure that Zavier wasn't back into his cheating ways, but the truth is that he never changed. Stan thought about everything that she's been through and decided not to tell her the truth. Instead he lied about what he really wanted to say. "I finally got a contract." He said trying to sound so convincing. "Okay, that's good...but what does that have to do with love and me?" I became even more puzzled as I was trying to figure out what was going on. "What I meant to say is that I have to leave today and that I love you and just don't want you to think that I don't care. That's all." He elaborated as he was still trying to sound persuasive. "Stanley, how long have we known each other? I know that you really care for me. Hell, you are the only person who really does at this point. I would never think of anything less or bad of you for whatever choice or decision you make." I responded and hugged him tightly. I could tell he felt relieved that I was okay with him leaving and I knew that this time was better than any to finally get everything off my chest. "You can stay here as long as you like. And I'm real cool with the neighbors so I'll have them watch out for you. The house has an alarm system and you can call me if you need anything." He said as he was holding my hand. "Thanks, Stan." I replied back. "But, wait you still gotta get cleared? Maybe, I can call them back and see if I can stay longer until you get that taken care of." Stan mentioned quickly as he grabbed his phone. "Hang up the phone and sit down." I scolded him like a mother would her son. "As soon as Eric made me the CEO of the law firm, he entrusted me with the company which gave me the clearance I needed to show that I was fully capable of being responsible for myself. I was just waiting for the right moment to throw it in his face and what better opportunity than this." I folded my arms after making my point. Stan couldn't help but smile and told me that Eric wasn't gonna like it. I knew he wasn't and that was the plan.

Since everything was falling right into place and I had the living arrangements taken care of, I figured it was my turn to get something off my chest. "Remember when you asked me why I went into the crazy house?" I asked Stan as he sat back down on the couch. "The asylum?" He said to correct me. "Same difference." I said as I waved my hand. "Well the night that I graduated, Zavier told me that he couldn't go out and celebrate because he had an early flight the next morning for a doctor's convention. So I told him that it was fine because I was going out with you and a few other people." I began refreshing his memory. "But, we didn't go out. Remember? I asked you, and you said that you and Zavier where going out of town. I'm confused." He replied. I told him that if he would just shut up and listen that he wouldn't be lost in the dark. He apologized and asked me to continue. "I lied to Zavier because I wanted to surprise him with....you know." I motioned my hands in a circle hoping Stan would get the idea. "Know what?" He was mocking me as he was motioning his hands like I did. "With it." I said as I stretched my hands out. "It what?" He replied by mocking me again. I blew my breath straight up into the air to announce my frustration with him. He started laughing and mentioned the next time I needed to do that, make sure I had a mint in my mouth. I ignored what he said, but I was glad that he could still find humor in the most difficult and awkward moments. "Sex Dammit!" I yelled. "Oh, you was gonna give ol' Zav the good good. You bad girl you." He said with a smirk as he gave me the shame gesture. I hit his hand and he promised that he was done talking. I then informed him that when I got to Zavier's house, I saw a car in the driveway. So, I was thinking maybe he had one of his colleagues visiting. After all, he was a popular doctor so that really wasn't something unusual; However-er when I opened the door, I found him and some girl on the living room floor butt naked. Stan asked me if I could see who she was. I told him no and that the only thing that I saw was weave, his ass and her back. I didn't wanna see any more I just knew I had to get outta there. "You never told me this. Why didn't you tell me this from the beginning?" Stan asked me. "I don't know. I felt embarrassed and stupid." I responded as the tears began to fall. "You're not stupid. You fell in love with a man who was old as dirt and you thought that with his age that it would be different." I rolled my eyes at Stan because he was trying to be funny. Zavier was only eight years older than me. "So, what does he cheating have to do with you and the asylum?" He asked still in a state of confusion. "Well, Stan, you know that I have trust issues and you know I grew up in foster care. When I saw Zavier with that woman, it caused me to think that I was unwanted and unloved. A "breakdown" was my diagnosis." I then showed him my wrists. He was astonished as he wanted to know the details of what happened. I didn't say a word to him. "Kaitlyn why would you try to....' He couldn't finish his sentence. I agreed that it was stupid and I wasn't thinking. "Promise me that you will call me if anything happens! I don't care what time it is or what I'm doing. Call me. I can't lose you. Just the thought of you even thinking about..." He grabbed my arm and put it around his neck. I wrapped the other one around it as well. I don't think he has ever held me this tight. He was holding me as if it was our last time. We had a heart to heart moment and it felt so good. But, Zavier cheating was only the half of it. I still couldn't really tell him the entire truth. In that moment, I forgot about Keith. I told Stan that I would cancel so I could spend more time with him. "No, Keith seems like a nice guy. He protected you and plus he called to check on you." I finally admitted that Keith was an okay guy and that I was interested in getting to know him better. "Now, tell Keith he better treat you right or he'll have to answer to me." He warned me while poking out his broad, chiseled chest. "Ugh, you might wanna rethink that. He's actually

kind of bigger then you." I said as I could imagine Stan trying to challenge Keith. "Only in height." Stan said with his chest still poked out.

I called Keith to ask if we could just do dinner and not lunch. He asked if everything was okay. "Yeah, I just need to get some clothes and a little bit more rest." I assured him. "Hey, if it's too soon we can do it another time." Keith said. "No, I'm fine. Going out will be good for me. I need to keep my mind occupied." I teasingly responded. "Is 8:00 okay for our date?" I was quiet for a moment when Keith said that. "Hello?" He asked again. "Date?" I questioned his use of the word. "Yeah, I think that it's safe to say that we are having our first date." He told me with such confidence in his voice. Sure, why not I thought to myself. I agreed 8:00 was perfect and he then asked where he could pick me up. I asked Stan if it was okay for Keith to pick me up at his place. He stated only if I felt comfortable. I did feel very comfortable with Keith because he saved my life. How could anyone not be comfortable with someone like that?

As I was sitting across the table from Keith, I couldn't help but wonder what was going through his head. Was he going to ask what Eric and I were talking about that night at the hospital? I wasn't prepared to tell a guy that I was starting to like that my ass was just released from the mental institution. "I'm really glad you decided to go out on a date with me." He said as he sipped his water. "Who the hell said that this was a date? We are just two people having dinner." He smiled as he knew I wasn't going to admit that this was actually a date. "You put on this front that you are such a bad ass and really what I see is a beautiful, sexy, attractive, young woman. Who deep down, is sweet, kind, lovable and kissable." Keith replied with a smirk as he was stared in my eyes. I knew he wanted me to comment on the kissable part, but instead I just changed the conversation. "Thanks for saving me." I said to Keith. "I'm just glad that I got there in time and you shouldn't have been hard headed in the first place." He winked to let me know he was joking. "So, tell me about yourself." I quizzed him when I realized that I really didn't know much about him. "Didn't we have this conversation already?" He replied. "Yes, but refresh my memory, if you don't mind sir?" I politely asked. As he started to tell me about himself again and how he started his traveling agency business, my cell phone rang. I excused myself from the table because I thought that it was Stan calling to check on me. If only I had known who it was I wouldn't have answered.

"Where the hell are you?" Eric bellowed in my right ear. "I'm busy right now. I'll have to call you back later." I screamed right back. "Kaitlyn, you are one step away from going back to the mental institution." Eric threatened. "Look, you bastard. I don't care who in the hell you call. They can't do a damn thing to me, okay? And, I have you to thank for that." I was still screaming as I had walked outside to further give him a piece of my mind. Then, there was complete silence on the line. I could hear Cassandra in the background yelling for Eric to come look at something. She then asked if he was talking to me and he lied and responded no, and he was on an emergency business call. "You bitch. I'm gonna get you. I promise you that. You think this is over, but it's just getting started." He threatened me once more. I quickly hung up the phone not wanting to listen to anything else he had to say. I wasn't gonna let him ruin my good night with Keith.

After Eric convinced Kaitlyn that he didn't know anything about her plan, he called Zavier. "Honey, how much longer are you gonna be on the phone?" Cassandra asked Eric before he could dial the number. "I have one more important phone call, alright? Fifteen minutes I promise, and then I'm all yours." Eric said as he kissed Cassandra and waited for her to make it upstairs before calling Zavier. "Where are you?" Eric asked Zavier. "I'm handling some business right now." Zavier said. "Whatever the hell you doing can wait. Listen, I just got off the phone with Kaitlyn. She's probably with Stan out somewhere considering that he's the only person that she trusts right now. So

I need you to call her like right now." Eric instructed Zavier. "I can't right now. I'm taking care of something very important. I'll just go see her at work tomorrow. I know she'll be there." Zavier informed Eric. "Aight, man, whatever.. I just need you to be getting closer to her. We are on a schedule and it's already three weeks behind." Eric said as he peeped out the door to double check that Cassandra hadn't come down. "Man, don't worry. I got this." Zavier reiterated as they ended their conversation.

Zavier laid the phone back down on the night stand and waited for Carmen to finish giving him head under the cover. He forced her mouth all the way down on him in order for him to cum. Once he ejaculated, he made sure that it went straight into her mouth. "We gonna have to cancel our plans for this week." Zavier revealed to Carmen as he went into the bathroom to clean himself. "Why?" She retorted with a furious look. "Baby, listen you know why. I'm doing this for the two of us. Don't you realize that?" He replied while returning into the bedroom. "Don't you mean the three of us?" She said as she heading to the bathroom. "What? No, I'm not doing this for Kaitlyn. I don't care for her baby, I care about you and only you." He persisted. "Wow! God, you can't be that slow. Really?" Carmen requested to know as she was leaning on the bathroom door. Zavier was looking confused as he was really clueless to what she was trying to say. "I'm pregnant. I'm guessing maybe four to six weeks, but I'll know once I go to the doctor next week." She notified him as she sat next to him on the bed. "Wait, you're what? How did this happen?" Zavier quickly questioned. "I guess you really are dumb if you don't know how two people can make a baby." Carmen responded as she slipped on her dress. "Don't sass me. You were on birth control. So, I'm not understanding how this is even possible." He was furious. "I stopped taking those depo shots last year. Baby, they were making me fat and since we're gonna be together anyway, what's wrong with adding another member to our family?" Carmen responded nonchalantly as she wrapped her arms around Zavier's waist. He unwrapped her arms and shoved her so hard that she had to grab the dresser to keep herself from falling. "What the hell is your problem, Zavier?" Carmen hollered. "Get rid of it and I'm serious. I don't care how, I don't care how much, but by tomorrow I want it gone." Zavier shouted as he ran downstairs and out of the house. Carmen had a plan of her own in mind, and getting rid of their unborn child wasn't one.

CHAPTER 7

As Keith was walked me to the front door of Stan's house, I realized how much I enjoyed our date and getting to know one another. I also realized that Stan was gone and I didn't know when he would be return. I wanted to spend more time with Stan, but he refused. I was pissed that he wouldn't let me say goodbye, but also knew why he forced me to go out. He knew that saying goodbye to each other face to face would have been too much for me and him. "I meant to tell you earlier when I picked you up how nice your house is." Keith interrupted my thoughts as he admired the house. Oh, this is Stan's house. He's letting me stay here for a while until I get my own." I responded as he was nodded his head stated that I had a good friend. Stan was more than my friend. He was my brother and my protector and now with him gone, I don't know how I was going to survive. You would think that three years in the nut house wouldn't make me miss Stan, but it did. I sat down on one of Stan's porch chairs holding my mouth. "Kait? What's wrong? Did I say something to upset you?" I shook my head no to Keith as I was still holding my mouth. I tried to keep silent and not let the deep

breath of air escape as I cried. I did my best until
I started choking on the air that was trying to escape. "Kait, Kait, come here." Keith beckoned while
he stretched his arms out for comfort. I shook my
head no as I reassured I was fine. He grabbed my
hands and placed them around his stern waist. "Shh...
It's gonna be okay. Whatever it is, it's gonna be fine.
I'm here and I won't leave until you want me to."
His voice soothed me while he rubbed my head. I
held onto him so tight, but he was holding me even
tighter and that made me feel safe again. "Let's get
you some water and something to wipe your face." He
said to me and I agreed that all of that crying made
my throat dry.

I invited Keith in for a second. I offered him a
seat, but he refused. I guess he didn't want me to
think that he was trying to get fresh with me. At
this point, I was so emotional that I wanted him to
take advantage of me. I went to go clean myself up
before I returned to Keith. I hoped the entire time
I cried, I didn't have any boogers hanging from my
nose. When I returned, I was surprised to see Keith
still in the same spot. "You okay?" He asked. "Yeah, I
was just having a moment. I apologize." I replied and
he grabbed my hands again. "Don't be. You've gone
through a lot and you're still standing." He said as he
kissed my hands and told me goodnight, but I wasn't
ready for him to leave. I pulled his hands back toward me and motioned for him to close the door.
He hesitated unsure if I was serious, so I closed the
door. I placed his hands around my curvy waist and
placed both my hands around his neck. We stared in

each other eyes for about a second before he realized what I wanted him to do. He removed his hands from my waist and placed them on my cheeks as he leaned in to kiss me. He teased me as he kissed me with his lips and then I felt his tongue as it slowly slipped into my mouth. I slightly opened it but realized that his tongue wanted me to open wider. Keith tongue was fat and I expected the kiss to be sloppy but it wasn't.

Before I knew it we ended up on the couch. He was on top of me and kissed my neck and caressed my thighs with his big, strong hand. I started to unbutton his shirt, but when I couldn't get it unbuttoned, I ripped it open. He was now on top shirtless showing his well-toned body. He kissed me all over as he started with my head, my lips, my chest, my breast, my thighs, my legs, and my feet. It felt all so good. I felt his hands go up my dress to pull down my black lingerie panties. I stopped him and looked at him with concern. He left them on and just went another route and the route was pulling them to the side. His tongue touched my pearl and it was feeling so good. I couldn't believe what actually happened. He caught me off guard so quick when he did it I let out a small sigh. I grabbed his head as I felt his tongue going in and out as his finger massaged my pearl. He knew he was hitting the right spot as I squeezed his head and started to moan louder. With my legs locked around his head, he fingered and licked me in all the right spots. I never knew four play could feel so good. I didn't even know how long he was down there. I just knew that he made me cum two times with an arch in my back. I pulled him back up to taste what made him hard. I then started to un-fasten his belt. I was so ready to feel what that bulge in his pants felt like until I screamed, "STOP! STOP! STOP!" It went from Keith to the face of my attacker in a matter seconds. One minute I was getting plea-sured and ready to give it up, and the next I'm fight-ing for my life. "I'm sorry. I'm sorry." He apologized as he got up. "No, it's me. I thought that I was ready and I'm not. I should be sorry for leading you on." I told him. "Don't be sorry. I shouldn't have stayed and maybe none of this would have happened." He told me as he picked up his shirt from the floor. We both apologized and tried to blame ourselves for what just happened until I finally told him that we both played a part in the situation. "I agree, but still it's more my fault then yours." He blamed himself as he was walked towards the door. I didn't disagree because I knew that the conversation would continue to go back and forth as we played the "blame game". Af-ter we finished, I told him goodnight and asked if he would kiss me one last time before he left. He agreed to kiss me, but only on my forehead because he ad-mitted that kissing me again would make him want to continue where we left off. I asked him to call me tomorrow and he promised he would before he re-minded me I owed him a shirt.

    Keith waved goodbye to Kaitlyn one last time be-fore he got into his car and answered his phone. "I thought I told you not to call me unless I called you." He responded flatly. "Yes, she's at Stan's house. No, he left for his football stuff. I'm handling this. I know what my job is. Never call me again unless I call you first." Keith looked into his rearview mirror to see if Kaitlyn was outside. She continued to wave goodbye and he blew his horn at her as he pulled off.

Before I could pick up the phone in my office my cell phone rang. "Wassup?" Stan said on the other end. "Hey, Stan." I was so glad to hear his voice. I wasn't shocked that he called as he was gone only one day "So, you do know why I called right?" He asked. "Yes, you want to know how the date went and if we had sex." I answered sarcastically. "Say what? I didn't know that you was gonna try to give him the cookie so soon. You know what they say? Once you go white you know you've been done right." I heard him chuckle. "Shut the hell up. And, I thought it was, once you go black you never go back." I corrected him. "Hell, that too. In this case it's the other way around." He said as he laughed again. "He was a gentlemen and I wasn't going to give him the cookie. I just know how yo mind be sometimes." I said while laughing, too, I then changed the subject and asked how he liked it in California and he said that the weather was great. "Let me know when your first game will be and I will be sure to come and watch." I requested. "Why wait 'til first game? Why not come out this weekend?" He stated. I turned around in my chair and faced my bookshelf as I thought about whether or not I should go. "I'll think about it." I told him. "Aight, baby girl. I gotta go. Call me if you need anything." He said in order to remind me that he was still there for me even though he was miles away.

"I thought I was the only man in your life." Zavier said as he walked in my office. "How do you know that it was a man?" I asked him. "Please, babe. You were either talking to Eric or Stanley, but considering you have a smile on your face I bet money that it was Stanley." He said as he approached my desk. "Anyway, what do you want?" I said as I was focusing my eyes on the computer. Zavier was walking around my desk and was kissing me on my cheek. "You know what I want." He said as he turned my chair around to try to kiss my lips. "Please stop and go away." I said as I pushed him back and got up from my chair. "You were supposed to call me and we were gonna talk about us." He said as stood by my chair. "Zavier? There is no us. After you left I thought about it and there is no way in hell that I will ever trust you again." I was very adamant this time, but his face wasn't convinced. "So, you didn't feel anything the other day when we kissed?" He asked. "No, I didn't and that was a mistake." I replied as I tried not to remember the feeling of us kissing. "By the way, who was that white guy in your hospital room? Why was he there anyway? I mean where the hell did he come from?" Zavier shouted out so many questions that I just covered my ears. I was glad he got off the subject of us, but I wasn't ready to explain Keith to him. "Baby, baby. I'm sorry. I just don't want nobody taking advantage of you okay. I love you too damn much to let anything else happen to you. I feel so bad already that I wasn't there to protect you that night." He rubbed my arms while I still covered my ears. He just had to ruin my day. "I mean, baby, to even think about anyone hurting you or doing something to you. I just can't imagine my life without you. Not now. Not when I'm trying to make things right. I was stupid and I was a jerk back then. You were so good to me and I just abused it. And I'm sorry. All I want is another chance, baby...please." He begged as he got down on his knees. I was still quiet until I heard a sniff and that's when I realized that he was crying. I'd never in my life seen this man cry. We dated for four years and even when his mom passed, he didn't shed a tear. I could tell that Zavier was beating himself up about the attack, but mostly for breaking my heart. "Zavier, stop. What happened to me could have happened to anyone. Besides it's my own fault. I shouldn't have been at the office that late anyway. " I said as I massaged his shoulders to let him know that I was concerned about him. "I had already forgiven you for cheating and I know you want us to pick up where we left off, but were we left off wasn't at a good place." I told him as I kept massaging him shoulders. "But, baby we can try? Please can't we try? Let's try." He pleaded and whispered as he got up and kissed me on my neck. Hot damn! He kissed my spot. Although Keith had kissed me there, he didn't kiss me in my spot like Zavier did right about now. "Zavier, stop for a second." I said as he had me laid flat on the couch with my hand rubbing his well-waved head. He knew kissing my spot made me weak and I was kind of mad at him for it, but not really. "Baby, I want you right here. Right now." He lifted up my skirt as he spoke to me. I wanted him, too, but I knew it wasn't the time or the place for us to be doing this. With all the strength I had left, I finally pushed Zavier off of me. "We gotta stop." I said to him with shortness in my breath. "Why? We can lock the door, the blinds are already closed. No one is gonna come in here." He expressed to me and pointed towards the door. "I know that, but this isn't the time or the place. Do you think that I really want my first time to be in my office?" I asked him. Zavier looked at me strange when I made that comment. I asked why he made that face at me. "Wait, you're still a virgin?" He questioned. "Ugh, yes. That night you cheated I had planned to give in to you, but obviously you had other plans. I've been in the crazy house for the past three years and I haven't even been out of it for a year. So, yeah, when have I had time to give somebody the cookie?" I laid it all out to him while I was stretched out on my back the reason I was still a virgin. After he heard this top-secret information, Zavier quickly bum rushed me and pinned me up against the wall and started kissing my spot again. "Ah, baby its meant to be. I wanna be your first. I wanna make love to you." He said passionately and kissed me harder. The emotions got the best of us as he lifted me up in the air and I wrapped my legs around him. My temperature rose immediately as I forgot everything that was previously said. He carried me over to my desk and shoved all the papers on the floor. I didn't care; I wanted him just as much as he wanted me. We tried to be as quiet as we could, but I knew that wasn't going to happen. Thankfully I heard a knock at the door. "Ignore it." Zavier said as kissed my stomach. "I can't." I mumbled as I tried to move his head up. "Just one taste, baby." He said finally pulled my panties down. "One second." I forced out as Zavier sucked on my pearl. It felt even better the second time. Damn, is this what I've been missing? "Okay, baby you gotta stop. Someone's at the door." I whispered as he held on tight to my thighs. "No. Not until you cum." He slurred as he licked me. I was focused hard on what Zavier was doing because his grip on me was tight and I knew he meant what he said. "Just one more second." I shouted to whomever stood on my door. And in fact, it really was another second before I was cumming in Zavier's mouth. When he tasted my cum, he made he had his whole entire mouth over it in order to catch all the juices. "Shit!" I yelled out before realizing how loud it was. "Tonight! My house for dinner." He instructed as he licked his lips. I was puzzled as to what had just happened and tried to get myself together. I opened the door let him out and motioned for the paralegal to come in. "Are you okay?" He asked. "Yes, I'm fine. Why?" I replied. "Well, because you look a little distraught and your papers are all over the floor." He pointed out. I had completely forgot about the papers and told the paralegal that I was upset about a case pertaining to the gentleman that he just saw. I believe that he bought it considering the fact that everybody knows that I don't like to lose.

As I soaked in the hot bubble bath, I imagined the night with Keith again in my head. Now, you would think that I would be imagining Zavier, but I was feeling horny tonight and Keith just so happen to pop in my head. I wanted him so bad that it was making me hornier and I had to do something about it. So, I did what any woman would do in her time of need. I took my middle finger and went to work. The entire time I imagined that it was Keith who pleasured me instead of myself. It worked for the purpose at hand, but I was still horny because my body knew that it was just a teaser and not the real thing. I pondered whether I should call Keith or not. He did say that it didn't matter who called who first because he knew that I had a busy schedule. I decided to give him a call. No one answered. I didn't leave a message because I figured he would call me back once he saw the missed phone call.

I stayed up for a while after getting out of the tub to go over my case in the morning hoping that he would call me back before I went to bed. I had been up well past the time I wanted to stay up so I decided to call it night. Just as I got prepared for bed my phone rang. Even though I didn't recognize the number I answered it anyway. "Hello?" I didn't hear anyone so I was about to end the call. "I thought you were coming over." Zavier said. I looked at the clock and saw that it was little bit pass ten and told him that it was too late. "It's not that late." He said. "Yes it is, and I have to be in court in the morning." I responded. "Okay, well what if I come over there. You can sneak me in and Cassandra and Eric won't even know I'm there." He said with a snicker. I had to stop and think for a minute if I wanted to tell Zavier that I didn't live there anymore. I was actually shocked that Eric hadn't told him just for the simple fact that they are best of friends. "What do really you want?" I asked in aggravation. "You know what I want. I wanna feel you cum in my mouth again. I wanna taste you. I wanna give you this." He said. I asked him what he wanted to give me as if I could really see what he was talking about. "Check your phone." He requested. I told him to hold on as I checked, and when that picture popped up on my phone, I thought it was a third arm. "Did you get it?" He impatiently asked. I did get it but, I couldn't respond because I was too busy looking at it to see if it was real "Kait? Kait?" He asked again. "Yeah, I'm here. Um, look its late and..." He interrupted and started telling me more things that he wanted to do to my body. It was bad enough that I was already horny and then he had to talk dirty, too. Ugh, his dirty talk worked because I told him to text me the directions to his house while I scrambled to try to find my sexy panties.

As I pulled in the driveway, Zavier was standing outside waiting for me. The reflection of the moon shimmered down in the water as I walked by and up the steps to Zavier's house. "Nice house, love the lake scenery." I said while I admired the view. "Well, I remember how you said you always wanted a house by the beach." He reminisced as he pointed to the lake. "Nigga, that ain't no damn beach." I replied and squinted in the direction he pointed. "No, it's not. It's better than the beach, and do you know why?" He tested me again. "No, why?" I retorted. "Because there's no one around and it's all mine." He pulled me close and kissed me. I really wanted Zavier true enough, but he was gonna have to work a little harder than that if he wanted this cookie. "So, you just wanted me to come over so that you can hit it, right?" I asked before I pulled myself away. "Well, that and because I want us to be together." He answered and looked down at his member as it was fully extended out. I chuckled a little as he tried to follow me into the house with his hard on. "Can't walk?" I spoke up. "What do you think?" He looked down and pointed to it. "C'mon." I welcomed him into the house as he stood in the doorway. I still couldn't believe I was going to experience sex for the first time-ever. I welcomed Zavier this time as he went for my spot again. He kept going like I wanted him to; he did that and more! "I'm gonna make love to you." Zavier proclaimed as he picked me and carried me upstairs. I tried helping him as I took my clothes off, but he pushed my hands back and told me to relax. I moaned as he kissed one of my breast and was squeezing the other one with his hand. "You like that?" He put his fingers inside me before I answered his question. I grabbed his hand and tried to control it, but he stopped. When he stopped, he grabbed both my hands and raised them over my head and held them down with one hand while his other hand went back to what it was doing. "Mmmmm......" I moaned like I smelled something good. He knew that I was well off into it, and that's when he caught me off guard and surprised me with the "D". "Oww..." I whispered as he tried to put more in. "Relax, baby." He still had my hands in his and pushed deeper. I tried to relax as much as possible, but it was just hurting too bad. "Zavier, please stop. It hurts." I begged him while at the same time trying to break free from his super strong grip. He told me that it would only hurt for a second and then it would start to feel good. I waited as long as I could for it to start feeling good, but it was just hurting more and more as he kept pushing it in deeper and deeper. "Zavier! Stop! Get off of me! Get off of me!" I yelled as I tried again to break from his death grip. At first he wasn't moving and still tried to get me to relax, but I started to cry and he eventually removed himself. "I'm sorry, baby. I just wanted you to enjoy it." He respectfully stated. "I think that I should go." I began to put my clothes back on and avoided eye contact. "No, baby, please stay. I'm sorry if I was pressuring you. Please stay. You can sleep in the other room if you want to." He said as he got dressed, too. "We're moving way too fast, and if there was even a chance of us getting back together, then we would need to go as slow as possible." I made sure that I articulated this correctly. "So, are you saying that you wanna be with me?" He frowned after what he heard me say. "Right now, I'm not sure. But, I will take it into consideration. Just know you are going to have to start all over from scratch. You are going to have to earn my trust back." I advised him before I headed downstairs. He kept saying that he was gonna prove himself to be worthy to me and that this time things were going to be different. I sure hoped he meant every word he said, because I had feelings for him again and I wanted us to work things out. Besides, no one is perfect and it was just that one time. I was able to forgive him for that. "I'll call you sometime tomorrow." I said before I opened the door. He kissed me again, but slowly and gently. "Drive safe and let me know when you've made it home." He sounded very concerned as he closed my door after I climbed into the car. I was unsure of what would happen next, but I felt like things were finally turning around for me.

CHAPTER 8

I heard my phone ring, but I couldn't find it. It sounded as if it was muffled under something, so I got down on all fours and lifted up the comforter to look for it. "Hello?" I answered. "Damn, what took you so long?" Stan asked. "Last time I checked you were not my daddy and I don't have one either." I hollered my response at Stan. "Don't say that. I know Eric can be an ass, but he still is your father." Stan tried to correct me. I responded nonchalantly and asked what he wanted because I was trying to get ready for work. "Well, I just wanted to check on you to make sure you were okay. I was notified that there had been some activity going on." He replied with a cough. "Are you spying on me?" I asked angrily as I rushed out of the door. "No. I told you one of my neighbors about you, and he called me to tell me that you seemed upset one night and that you weren't alone but you left later on that night." He said with concern. "What? You told your neighbor my business. Why in the hell would you do that? I was beyond livid. Okay first of all, I can go get me an apartment now. Next, I am grown and don't need nobody watching me." I shouted at Stan and hung up the phone in his face. I was really glad that I didn't invite Zavier over because if Stan knew that, he would have a fit. I wasn't that type of woman to disrespect anyone's home that wasn't my own.

As I arrived to the office, I saw Cassandra standing outside of the courthouse. "Hey." She greeted me with a sad look on her face. "Hi." I replied. "Sorry, I didn't come to the hospital that night. I wanted to but your father insisted that I stay home because I was emotional." She elaborated and followed me into the courthouse. "He's not my father and why are you bringing this up? That happened weeks ago." I disclosed this information, just in case she forgot, as we waited for the elevator. "I know and I should've called, but I just didn't know what to say." Cassandra stated and then looked away in shame. "How about asking if I was okay, or how I was doing? Of course those would have been stupid questions to ask, but at least it would've showed that you cared. At least that's what you tell me all the time. You care, right?" I rolled my eyes at her while we walked to my office. "Was it something else you needed? Because I do have to be in court in the next twenty minutes." I was ready to get rid of her. "Right. I just wanna make sure that you didn't forget your Grandmother's birthday party that's coming up." She reminded me. "Ah, gee. I forgot to tell you that I already promised Stan that I would visit him." She looked at me confused, like she knew I was lying. "Well, can you go this week instead?" Cassandra forcefully asked. "Nope, because I've taken on a case load this week and I really need to concentrate on those." I responded halfheartedly and continue to prepare my documents for court. I waited for her to leave, but it seemed like she had something else to ask. I didn't give her the opportunity as I picked up the phone to page Carmen to get my itinerary for the day. Five pages later, she still didn't answer. I paged the other receptionist. "Amanda, why isn't Carmen at her desk? I paged her like five times already and she hasn't responded." I was very upset with her by this time. "No, one has seen her Ms. Thomas." Amanda quickly responded by speakerphone. I don't have time for this right now I said to myself. I instructed Amanda that she was going do Carmen job for the day and I was to be notified as soon as Carmen got in.

I sat at my computer and hoped that Cassandra would get the idea that I was very busy, and make a beeline for the door. She kept trying to convince me to attend the party. "Cassandra, I just can't, okay. I understand that you would like for me to be there, but I don't belong there." I answered in a distracted tone as I responded to my emails. "What do you mean you don't belong there? You're a part of our family despite the fact that I'm not your real mother." Cassandra answered me in a hurt tone. "Well, I won't pressure you. That is the last thing that I wanna do right now." She said. "Okay, I really appreciate that and I am sorry, but I really have to get ready for court." I interrupted her and gathered my case files. She understood and headed for the door, but turned around to tell me something else. "I know that you don't believe me, but I really do love you like you were my own flesh and blood." Cassandra's voice quivered as she responded. I didn't even look up at her as she left, I was just glad that she was gone. I haven't heard from this lady in weeks and then out the blue here she is. Not that I care if she's around or not, it's just the simple fact of her telling me how much she cared and yet she never came to see me in the crazy house, nor had she been checking up on me to see how I was adapting. I know that bastard Eric won't do it because if he could have his way, I would be there and instead of here right now. "Ms. Thomas, you're due in court in ten minutes." Amanda's voice over the loud speaker interrupted my thoughts. Saved by the bell was all I could say to myself because it quickly took my mind off of the situation at hand.

It had been a very stressful day. I really needed a drink. The club that Stand and I went to popped in my head, but I didn't have a clubbing buddy. I wasn't planning on going alone especially after my attack. I was trying to think why I still haven't heard from Keith yet. I called him once yesterday and he hasn't called back yet. I tried calling once more before I got ready to go home and nothing. I did decide to leave a message in hope that he would call me right back:

"*Hey, Keith it's me Kaitlyn. I know you're probably busy, but I just wanted to let you know that I enjoyed our date and hope we could see each other again. And, don't worry about what happened the other night it wasn't you at all. You were wonderful. Okay, I think I've talked too much. Call me whenever. Okay, bye.*"

I had my pepper spray and taser ready for the next bastard who wanted to try me. As I walked outside to my vehicle, I realized I wasn't alone. There Zavier stood right by my car. "I wanted to make sure that you got home safe." He said as he approached me. "I thought you worked nights at the hospital?" I asked him. "I do, but I took my break late so that I could make sure that you got home safe." He replied. "So, now you're stalking me?" I grilled Zavier as he held my car door open so I could get in. "No, Kaitlyn. I just wanna make sure that nothing like......I just wanna keep you safe." I could tell he was truly genuine with his words and that he really wanted to keep me safe. "Well, I'm safe so goodnight." He grabbed my door before I could close it and ask if I wanted to get something to eat. "Zavier, it's midnight. There isn't a restaurant open this time of night." I stated in a matter of fact tone as I waited for him to close my car door. "I picked up some food on my way here because I figured that you wouldn't have a chance to eat." He hesitated. I was hungry and didn't wanna cook so I asked for the food. "What am I gonna put it on, babe?" He replied with a silly chuckle. I forgot where we were for a second, and he invited me back to his house and all I could think was not again. "Just to eat. Don't think you getting any ass tonight just because you bought me dinner." I answered as I slammed my car door.

My phone buzzed as I was following Zavier to his house. I pushed the talk button on my steering wheel without looking because we were almost at Zavier's house, and I knew it was him calling. "You're still not getting any ass no matter how you ask me." I yelled into the air. "Sorry, did I catch you at a bad time?" Keith asked Oh my God. I knew I should have looked down to see who it was before I answered and opened my huge mouth. "No, um, I thought that you were. Never mind. How are you?" I was embarrassed as I answered Keith's question. "I'm good and how are you?" He replied. I told him that all was well and reiterated him how much I enjoyed our date. "Me too. We should definitely do it again sometime." Keith answered in agreement. I confirmed with him once again that we were good and that I would like to see him again, too. He said that when he got back in town that he would be available at any time on any day. "The pleasure of being your own boss." I remembered that he had his own travel agency. "Don't worry. You'll get there one day. It just takes time and patience." He responded with such confidence. I really wanted to ask his whereabouts as I listened for a woman's voice in the background. "Hey, I gotta go. Give me a call as soon as you get back in town." I rushed Keith off the phone as Zavier approached my car. "Okay, talk to you then." Keith said as I quickly ended the call.

Zavier opened my car door and asked if everything was alright. "I'm good. Why?" I asked him with curiosity. "No reason at all." He replied nonchalantly as we walked to his house. I had a feeling that he knew I was on the phone but if he questioned it, I was simply gonna say that I was on the phone with Stan. That could be believable considering the fact that he is my best friend.

After dinner, Zavier offered me some coffee. I declined and informed him that coffee kept me from sleeping. I seriously needed to get some rest. "Well, you don't have to go home." He caressed my leg after that statement. Oh, no it's starting already. I quickly got up and put my shoes back on. "Thanks, but no thanks. I remember what happened last time I was here." I told him as I reached for my purse. "Baby, you gonna honestly say that you didn't enjoy our time together?" He wanted me to sit back down. "Yes, it was nice, but the sex." I paused as I was remembering how badly it hurt. "Why?" Zavier asked with a frown. "Why what?" I responded to his question with a question. "Don't get me wrong I love the fact that you are a virgin. But, why is it that you are still a virgin? When you wanted me to stop, I thought that you were just saying it and didn't mean it until you cried. Is there something that you're not telling me?" Zavier wondered as he made sure to lock eyes with me. "No, I just never was interested into being like everyone else and having sex because everyone was doing it. I wanted to save myself for someone special. I wanted my first time to be memorable." I educated him as I got up to pace the floor. He believed that part, but he still felt like I was holding something back because he said that there was fear in my eyes. "Now, you're just being ridiculous." I insisted. "Okay, I'll let you tell me when the time is right." He finally let it go.

I was thanking him for dinner and made my trek to the door. "Don't you gotta go back to the hospital?" I asked once I noticed that he wasn't leaving out with me. "I do, but I'm on call right how. So, I'm just gonna stay here and get some sleep before that pager start to go off." He pointed to it as it set on the living room table. "I'll call you once I get in." I yelled as I got in-to my car. I watched as Zavier watched me exit the driveway. I blew the horn to let him know that I was out of sight. Even though I was hoped we could work things out, I also looked forward to going out on another date with Keith. I didn't see anything wrong with me going out on a date with him. I mean after all, I was single.

Zavier closed the door as Kaitlyn left his house. He could tell that he was getting to her and that his plan was working. As he headed upstairs his doorbell rang. He rushed to get it because he knew that it was Kaitlyn coming back. "Baby, I'm so glad...." he stopped as he saw Carmen standing there. "You gonna let me in or what?" She demanded. "What the hell are you doing here?" He quizzed Carmen. "Are you gonna let me in or should I just get back in my car and follow Kaitlyn and tell...." He yanked Carmen in before she finished her threat. "Did you do what I told you?" Zavier interrogated Carmen as he poured himself a drink. "Well, that depends." Carmen replied with a smirk. "What the hell do you mean by that depends? Either you did what I asked or it's over." Zavier threatened her this time. Carmen laughed and cautioned Zavier to never threaten her like that again or she was going to expose him. He didn't seem worried until Carmen showed him a video with him and Eric. "Do you see that? That's you and Eric, and do you hear that?" She continued as the video played. "Oh, and you can take the phone and break it, but you better believe that I have copies." She informed Zavier. He paid close attention to the date of the video of when it was recorded and in fact it was a week before Kaitlyn's discharge. He felt trapped by Carmen and hated the fact that she had the upper hand. He knew that he had to come up with something fast and quick to keep Carmen happy and to make sure that Kaitlyn fell back in love with him

CHAPTER 9

As I waited for Stan to pick me up from the airport, I was still confused about my feelings for Zavier. I knew deep down that I was still in love with him, but the thought of him cheating again was something I didn't want to experience. I mean, it was partially my fault for wanting to wait until we were married to have sex. A man has needs and it was probably selfish of me to not take care of his needs, therefore he sought help elsewhere. I gotta try to not think about him this entire weekend because Stan will sniff it out like a dog sniffing a bone. "Kaitlyn?" A woman said as she tapped my shoulder. "Oh my God!" I shrieked as we hugged each other very tight. I was so excited to see my foster sister Alivia. We grew up pretty much together at the foster home. We got along so well because our birthdays were only nine days apart, and we didn't take any crap from anybody. We promised at one point that we would keep in touch, but we couldn't locate each other. Eric wouldn't help me find out who adopted Alivia after my adoption was final with them. That was another reason why I hated them so much. They kept me from my one and only friend. I was miserable until I met Stan. He made me laugh from the first thing he said which was, "Wassup, I'm Stan the man." From that moment forth we have been two peas in a pod. "How have you been?" I asked her as we let go of one other. "Well, I've been doing alright I guess. What about you? You are looking wonderful, honey." Alivia said as she examined me up and down followed by two snaps of her fingers. "Nothing much, on vacation right now." I said to her as I tried to call Stan to see what was taking him so long. "What are you doing here?" I replied. "Well, I just got back in town and I've been living here for about the past 5 years and before that I was living in Atlanta. Do you need a ride?" She extended an offer of transportation. "I don't wanna bother you. My friend was supposed to pick me up and I don't know where the hell he at?" I looked around the airport with disappointment. "Girl, it's no problem at all." I agreed to have her take me to Stan's Condo. I remembered the area where he told me he was living. I just hoped that he would answer his phone by the time I got over that way. "So, you married? Have kids?" She asked on our route to the car lot. "Oh, hell naw girl. I don't want no kids. I was supposed to be married, but that is another story I don't care to talk about." I told her. "Girl, me neither. Being in foster care does something to you as an adult. I date here and there, but I haven't really found that one guy who makes my heart melt or give me butterflies." I giggled and told her she sounded like a woman from a Lifetime movie.

I can still remember way back when she told our foster home mother, Ms. Cathy, that if she got a little ding a ling in her life, then she wouldn't be so bitchy all the time. I think that's why we got along so well. I could think it and she would say it. "Hey, what the hell happened to you picking me up?" I asked Stan when he finally answered his phone. "My bad I was at practice. I'm on my way now." He said. "Don't worry about it just text me your address." I hung up the phone in is face once again. I think he enjoyed aggravating me constantly. "I swear he can be annoying." I said to Alivia as I rolled my eyes. "So is this your boyfriend?" Alivia asked. "No, my best friend Stan." I told her. "Wait, I thought I was your BFF." She responded sadly with a frown. "You are in a way. You never stopped being my best friend even though we haven't seen each other in ages. Stan is just filling in." I said with a laugh. "Yeah, heffa. You cheating on me." We both cackled when she made that statement. "I wished that we could have gotten adopted together." I became sad as she pulled up to Stan's Condo. "I know right. But no one wants two grown ass girls with attitudes in their house." I agreed that she was right because we were both something serious. I saw Stan from the distance as I remembered the color and make of his Mercedes. I got out of the car and advised Alivia to get the hell outta dodge. She insisted that she wanted to meet the person who took her place as BFF. "Okay, girl, I warned you. The conversation will probably go like this: Wassup? I'm Stan the man and I've been thinking of a master plan and it includes you." Alivia couldn't believe her ears as I quoted Stan word for word as he introduced himself. He looked confused when she didn't laugh or even say something smart back to him. "Aight, enough she's not interested." I told Stan. "Yeah because you told her something negative about me probably." Stan retorted. "No. I just think that your so called pick up line is getting corny and old." I joked and winked at Alivia. "Oh really? So maybe I need to pick up a few pointers from Zavier then, huh?" I rolled my eyes at Stan as he stood there and grinned. He looked like he just got a happy meal.

Me and Alivia hugged once more and exchanged numbers. It was good to see her and knowing that she achieved her dream and became a physical therapist. There's not too many people in this world who know what they wanna do and then actually follow through with it. I was proud of her and hoped that we could rekindle our friendship.

After a much needed rest from my long flight, I told Stan that I wanted to go party. Clubbing was like my therapy. I enjoyed the music and plus there was always that one guy who couldn't dance, that one girl with an ugly ass outfit, and a "who did that" hairdo. "Um, does Zavier know you got this on?" Stan asked me as I checked my reflection in the mirror one last time before we left. "Why do you keep bringing up his name?" I was so disgusted with him as I opened the door. "I'm just saying I don't want no ish started at this club." He told me as he locked the door. I must look damn good if he was making a big deal about my outfit. "You'll do. A dude might buy you a drink." He casually responded and made the okay gesture with his hand. I flipped him the middle finger and advised him to stop hating.

We ended up at a well-known Reggae Club in the big state of California. I was so excited that I didn't wait for Stan to come to the dance floor. My jam was playing once again and it was also the song that Keith and I danced to. I couldn't get Keith out of my head while I was dancing so I decided to order me a shot and find Stan. It wasn't hard to find him considering he was the only big swollen dude with a yellow shirt on looking like Big Bird. "This is VIP." The wannabe cop said as he put his hand up letting me know I wasn't getting in. "Really? I didn't know that Sherlock." I tried to push past him, but his fat ass wouldn't budge. "Ma'am, you don't have the wrist band to get in so you need to walk your ass back down the stairs." He warned me as he tried to push me down the steps. Who does this big, black wanna be cop think he is by putting his hands on me? I don't give a damn how big he is. I will kick him in the nuts and then two shots to the nose.

"Yo, yo. She's cool. She's with me." Stan's voice bellowed as he ran and stood in between me and this ugly ass rental cop. Stan grabbed my hand as I flinched at the rental cop and told him if he was feeling froggy to leap. He laughed, but I was so serious. "Will you bring yo' crazy ass on. I think you need to lay off the Tequila. Why don't you try a daiquiri?" Stan suggested as he summoned the waitress over. I took my shot to the head and demanded that he order me two more. I knew how Tequila made me feel and act, so I took his suggestion of a baby drink into consideration. I didn't wanna embarrass Stan in front of his football buddies. I told him that I would have a margarita considering the fact that I was already drinking white.

The DJ went way back when he played the song, "Murder She Wrote." One of Stan's team mates asked me to dance. I didn't mind because for whatever reason Stan never danced. At least in front of me he didn't. I was grinding on ol' boy as I sang the chorus. "Damn, girl." He pulled back a little hoping I didn't feel his hardness, but it was too late. I was enjoying myself until some asshole asked to cut in. I turned around and it was Stan. "My bad, cuz, didn't know this was all you." His teammate said as they switched places. "I thought you didn't dance." I asked him and continue to wind my hips. "I didn't say that. You just assumed, but I didn't like how he was holding you and looking at you." Stan sounded very jealous. "Stan, how else do you dance with a gorgeous female like this?" I said as I turned around and put my hands around his neck to tease him. "I heard some things about that dude with women and I rather not go to jail tonight if that nigga try something with you." Stan informed me and wrapped his arms around my waist.

I closed my eyes for a moment to keep my balance and when I realized that didn't help, I decided to tough it out and open my eyes, but as I opened them I was looking at Zavier. I immediately started kissing him passionately as if we weren't in public. He was kissing me back and holding me tight. It was feeling so good until I rubbed his bald head. I pushed who I thought was Zavier away and realized that it was Stan. "Stan, I'm sorry. I think I've had too much to drink." I told him. "I'm not." Stan said as he tried to continue. "Stan, no really I thought you were Zavier. I'm sorry." I looked at him and realized his were hurt. "I didn't mean it like that. I'm just saying that we could never be together. You're like a brother to me and I don't think that I could see you like that. Plus, something sexual could ruin our friendship." I grab Stan's hand to assure everything was still good between us, but he jerked it away. "I think we should go." Stan mentioned to me. I didn't say anything to him the entire night because it seemed like everything I said just made the situation worse and made him feel bad.

As I felt the sun shining through the curtains on my closed eyes lids, I knew it was time to get up. I decided to take a really long hot bath hoping that it would help this hangover in some way. Just as I was got comfortable, my phone rang. I wanted to ignore it because I knew it was probably either Eric or Cassandra. Then the phone rang incessantly so I had no choice but to get up and answer it. I hesitated when I saw Zavier's name on the screen but then I saw that he had been calling me since early this morning. "Hello?" I answered. "Babe, where you been? I've been calling you all night. Are you okay?" Zavier sounded hysterical. "Zavier calm down. I'm fine. I'm surprised Cassandra, better yet Eric, didn't tell you where I was." I said in a state of shock. "No, I haven't talked to them recently. Where are you?" I really didn't want to tell Zavier where I was because of what happened last night between me and Stan. I knew that I shouldn't feel guilty, but for some reason I did. When I finally told him where I was, there were a million questions that followed. My head began to hurt, so I gave him an excuse that my phone was almost dead and that I would have to call him back. I didn't hear the last thing that he said because I ended the call. I didn't have the energy to deal with him at the moment. Besides, I had to save whatever energy that I had left to talk to Stan about last night.

"Good Morning." I said to Stan as I entered the kitchen. "Morning? It's twelve o' clock." He responded with such dryness. I hated how he was acting so I decided to bring last night up again. "Listen, I understand. I'm the guy who you can call on when you need help or need a laugh, but I'm not good enough to be loved." He responded emphatically as he left the kitchen. "Stan, that's not fair. I told you that I was sorry, okay? I don't know what else you want from me." I yelled out. "What I want? It's never about what I want. Everything is all about you." He shouted back. I didn't know where all this anger was coming from, but I've never seen him this upset with me before. I hope it was because he was nervous about his first official game, but Stan is never, ever nervous. I left him alone and went upstairs to find Alivia's number. I figured I give Stan some space and maybe later on he would have calmed down.

CHAPTER 10

I waited outside for Alivia to pick me and secretly hoped that maybe Stan would come outside and be annoying as usual to ask where I was going. He didn't and I knew then that he was still upset with me. "Hey girl." Alivia greeted me as I got in the car. "Hi." I replied back. "Uh, what's up with the attitude?" She asked. I began to tell her all about last night as we were heading to Sunset Blvd. "I see why he got mad at you." Alivia replied. "What do you mean you see? I didn't do anything wrong." "Isn't it obvious? He likes you more than just a friend." She expressed her opinion. I gave her a weird look and told her that we had known each other since childhood never once even tried to date each other. "I saw the way he looked at me and then the way he looked at you. He dates other women to keep his mind off of you and in reality, when you kissed him he thought you were finally feeling the same." She noted. "I thought you were a physical therapist and not a psychologist." I laughed at her when she tried to enlighten me on Stan when she's only met him once. I told her that I didn't wanna spend the entire day talking about Stan and his mood and that I rather spend time catching up on our lives.

Stan was only upset about last night a little, but what really got him was what he found out about Zavier. He didn't know how to tell Kaitlyn without her being mad at him for hiring a private investigator to spy on Zavier. So, he was caught in between on hiding a secret and telling the truth. "So, where is he now?" Stan questioned the investigator over the phone. "Right now, he's at home alone." The investigator informed Stan. "The woman isn't there?" Stan asked. "No, she's not here." He replied. "Okay, I want you to watch her as well and let me know what you find out about her." Stan hold him. "That's gonna be an extra three-hundred dollars per hour." The investigator updated him on the prices of his services. Stan, didn't care how much it was gonna cost. He only wanted to protect Kaitlyn and to keep her safe as promised.

I was enjoying our time as we were catching up on life and having some good laughs until Alivia noticed something. "What happened?" Alivia asked me. "Mm? What?" I said with a confused look. "Your wrist?" Alivia pointed out to me. I quickly pulled my arms back off the table and told her I fell and the cuts never healed properly. "I know my hair is blonde, but that doesn't make me dumb." Alivia was insulted by my desperate excuse. I informed her it really wasn't anything to worry about and I wanted to do a little bit more shopping before she dropped me off. She let it go, but gave me that look like she would beat my ass if I ever did it again. I knew she had figured out what happened because we were so much a like that we could be twins. But, I believe she just wanted me to say it and acknowledge what I did.

Overall, our time together was good and I hated the fact that I was leaving in just a few more days. We promised that we would see each other before I left and continue to stay in touch. "He's ready to talk." Alivia revealed to me as we said our goodbyes. I turned around to see that Stan was outside. I was glad to see him, but hesitant to talk to him. "Call me later." Alivia said as she reversed out of the driveway. It was then just me and Stan. He grabbed my bags and sat them in the house and closed the door before I could go in. "Walk with me." He ordered. I was nervous and anxious at the same time as we strolled down the street. It was quiet until Stan started talking. "I'm not mad at you. Okay?" He said to me. "Are you sure? Because you haven't said much to me lately." I replied as we continued to walk. Stan stopped and placed himself in front of me. "Listen, it's just that I thought maybe you thought about the possibility of us." He explained while he was holding my hands. I never thought about seeing Stan that way since we've known each other and I never knew he felt this way about me. I guess Alivia was right all along. "Stan, I've always saw you as my little brother and not anything more. And again I am sorry if that kiss made you feel otherwise. But, I just don't..." Before I could finish he had let go of my hands and went to rubbing his bald head. He asked me why not. Clearly, he didn't hear me the first time when I said that I didn't see him like that. So, for me to make it even clearer I told him that I've thought about getting back with Zavier. "What the hell is wrong with you?" He exclaimed. "Excuse me?" I said with a frown as we stood in the same place. "That nigga don't care about you. And the things that he..." Stan stopped himself he said too much. "Doesn't everyone deserve a second chance? It was my fault anyway." I said. "If a man can't respect the fact that you want to be celibate until marriage, then he's not the one for you." He uttered as he shook his head no. "What the hell do you know? Huh? You sleep with anything with a pulse." I shouted because I was now pissed off. Who the hell does he think he is to tell me how to live my life? "Kait! Kait!" Stan hollered as I walked faster down the street. I didn't want him to see me cry so I sped up as if I didn't hear him. He finally caught up to me and saw that I was crying. "Kait, I'm sorry. I didn't want to make you upset. I just wanna protect and keep you safe. That's all." He told me as he tried to hug me. I was still mad so I gave him a half of a hug instead of a full body hug. "Stan, you can't me protect all the time. I think that it's about time that I protect myself and not just depend on you to save me whenever I am in trouble." I reminded him as I wiped my eyes with my hands. I was really relieved that we were somewhat back on good terms. I knew that Stan meant well, but he just have to accept the fact that I was gonna make my own choices for what I wanted. "Well, I'm not gonna stand in your way of happiness." Stan said as we sauntered back to his house. "Thanks, I really appreciate that." I grabbed his hand to hold it, but he pulled it back. "Still mad?" I asked him. He told me that he wasn't mad, but just that holding hands was inappropriate for friends to do. I was getting pissed because we use to hold hands and hug all the time like it was nothing. "Well, I gotta get some rest because I have an early flight." I told him as he opened the door for me. "What time?" I told him that Alivia was gonna take me and not to worry. He didn't respond as he went into the kitchen and I went upstairs. I immediately texted Alivia and asked if she would take me to the airport. Of course, she agreed, and then she replied back and asked what happened. I told her that it was too much to text and that I would tell her what happened when she picked me up.

It wasn't until I looked out the window and saw we had landed back in Louisiana that I realized my vacation was over. I hated the fact of leaving, but I was glad to be home. I called Zavier to pick me up from the airport and told him that we needed to talk about a few things. He didn't have any idea that I was going to take him back, but since I am it is only fair for me to ask him to tell me anything that I don't know or any secrets that may come out later. Before, getting back with him I wanted to make sure that I knew everything that happened while we were together and the time we spent apart.

"Hey, babe" He smiled as he saw me coming towards him. "Hey." I said with such dryness. "What's wrong love?" He grabbed my luggage and searched my face for an answer. I told him that it was nothing and I just wanted to be alone with him. He was thrilled when he heard that and told me to wait by the curb as he got the car. I wasn't sure if it was the flight, or the eagerness to talk to Zavier, but all of a sudden I was felt queasy. "I thought that I wasn't supposed to see you until later on?" I turned around and there was Keith. Talk about being the monkey in the middle. "Hey, were you on my flight?" I inquired with a dumb look. "No, my plane landed about forty-five minutes ago. I was just waiting on a ride. Do you need a ride?" Keith asked as he tried to get closer to me. "No thank you. I have a ride already. Zavier's delivery was right on time as he pulled alongside the curb. "Well, can I ride with you?" Keith asked. I slowly moved away from Keith hoping that Zavier didn't see us talking, but apparently he did because he got out of the car and slammed his door shut. "It was nice seeing you again Kait." Keith said as Zavier opened my door. I replied with a smile not wanting Zavier to think that anything was going on between me and Keith. "How do you know my fiancée'?" I heard Zavier ask Keith as he closed my door. The thought of rolling down the window to correct Zavier came across my mind, but I didn't do it. I guess I wanted to see what Keith's reaction would be. "Um, didn't know she had a fiancée." Keith answered. "You didn't answer my question." Zavier replied boldly. "I'll let her tell you." Keith said with a smirk as he walked to the cab behind us. My heart was beating so fast that it almost felt like I was gonna have a heart attack. I enjoyed the thought of two men arguing over me even though I knew it isn't right. But, I just wanted Zavier to know that if he cuts up this time, that I had someone else who was willing to take his place.

The ride to Zavier's house was very uncomfortable. He indeed asked me about Keith and I just politely told him that he was just a friend. Of course he didn't believe me because he witnessed how Keith looked at me. I kept assuring Zavier that there wasn't anything going on with Keith, but friendship. "Well, I'm done talking about him. I want to talk about us." I said to get Zavier's mind off of Keith. "Go ahead." He said to me. "Well, while I was out of town I did a lot of thinking. I want to give us another try, but I need something from you in return." I told him. "Anything baby. Whatever it is." He said as he took my hand to kiss it. I suggested that we go inside to finish the conversation. In reality, I wanted another minute or two to really think about my decision to be with Zavier.

As we walked into the kitchen I leaned up against the sink thinking about what I was going to say. "Baby, you know I love you. And I never want to lose you again. My answer is yes to whatever it is you want." He pulled me close and kissed him. I tried to tug away but before I could, he picked me up and sat me on the kitchen counter. I kissed him back and tried to unfasten my pants at the same time. Zavier pulled my pants down along with my panties as I laid on the counter. As I felt his wet tongue and lips on me, I began to moan and squeeze his head. He was licking me in all the right spots. Zavier was making me feel so good that my body triggered my mouth to tell him that I loved him. It was too late to take it back as he came up and offered the same sentiments. I welcomed Zavier in me as he scooted me to the edge of the counter. I let out a sigh of relief once he was all inside of me. Once it was secured he told me to wrap my legs around him and to hold on. When I did as commanded, he then lifted me up and placed my body up against the wall. As my body went up and down against the wall, he told me again that he loved me. "I love you too." I moaned back. "Say it again." He instructed with each pump as I was up against the wall. "I love you...I love you. Yes! Yes! OH!" I groaned again. "Marry me. Marry me." He stated. I heard him and yet I couldn't respond, mostly because the sex felt so damn good. As I felt him slow down, I revealed that I couldn't marry him. I guess he didn't like my answer because he then carried me from the wall and bent me over the kitchen counter. "I want you and only you. Say you'll be my wife." He said to me with each pump as he was hitting me now from the back. I bit my lips together to hold in the scream that I wanted to let out. "I can't hear you." He said. "Oh my God!" I finally released. "That's not the answer." He said as he was smacking my ass with each hard pump. "Baby! Stop." I yelled to him in passion. "Say yes! Say it...say it......." He yelled back to me as I was cumming. "YES! YES! YES!" I screamed. "Ah...yeah." I heard him mumble as we climaxed together. They say good sex will make you do and say anything. I guess they were right because it was official at that moment; we were engaged again.

I waited for him to move before getting up to ask what the hell that was all about. The tension was so hot that we went upstairs to get in the tub to clean off to only make love again. "I told you that once you relaxed it would feel good." He said as I had just finished riding him. "Whatever. We can't do this all night. I gotta go to work in the morning." I informed him. "If you are able to walk." He said as he pulled my face down to kiss me. "I can't take anymore, baby." I mumbled in between the kisses. He ignored what I was saying and went to kissing my spot. Dammit! If this nigga don't stop doing that then I won't be going to work in the morning.

Zavier wasn't lying the night before when he said I wouldn't be able to walk. My legs were sore and she was too. Geez! He kept me wanting him, but we beginners needed a timeout or a tap out. But, the only real reason why I pushed myself to go to work was my need to talk to Keith. For some reason, I was scared to tell him that I was engaged. I don't know why, I mean it's not like we were dating. Even though we did come really close to having sex, I still didn't understand why I was so nervous. "Hey." I said as soon as Keith answered. "Wassup?" He responded "Wassup? You done went gangsta in just a few weeks I see." I laughed a little. "Nope, just really relaxed at the moment." He chuckled into the phone. "Listen, if you're not too busy today, would you like to have lunch?" "Sure. Around what time?" He answered eagerly. "Well, my next appointment isn't until three so how about twelve?" I asked him. "I get two hours? How much is this gonna cost me?" He said with a chuckle. "Well, if you looking for some counseling then it'll be $350 an hour, but if it's just two friends having lunch then it's free." I said. "Yep, can't afford you. I'll take the number two please." He said. I laughed at him and told him where to meet me for lunch. It was nice talking to Keith and he made me laugh. I just wished that I felt better about telling him the truth.

I heard a knock at my door and it was Carmen walking in. "So you're alive and well." I commented. "I'm sorry Ms. Thomas. I was having a family emergency with my boyfriend and I just had to...never mind, it won't happen again." She hesitantly stated. "Okay, well glad to hear that. I need these files pulled for my three o'clock appointment." I told her as I went back to looking at my computer screen. "Yes, Ms. Thomas." Carmen said as she took the paper. "Again, I'm sorry and it won't happen again." She repeated before she left office. I waved my hand at her to gesture "alright" as I took her word for it this time.

Keith must've been too excited to have lunch with me because he was already standing outside the restaurant. "Either you're super early or I'm super late." I said as he held the door open for me. "No, you're right on time. A gentlemen never makes a woman wait on him. A gentlemen waits on the woman." He sensibly replied as he pulled my chair out for me. Man, he was good. He didn't realize that he was making this even harder than it was already. I felt like he needed to know because I didn't want him to get the wrong idea about us. I mean, yes, at one point I thought I liked him and I was like two seconds from sleeping with him, but I was just emotional. If I slept with him, I probably would have regretted it for the rest of my life. "Keith, listen, I gotta tell you something." I began. "Okay? I'm all ears." He sat up straight and placed his full attention on me. "You're a really great guy and also nice. You make me laugh and you always know what to say." I continued. He said thank you and smiled back. "What I want to say. Is that I..." My phone started humming again. "I'm sorry." I told him. When I reached for my phone, I noticed the call was private. I usually don't answer private calls, but I remembered that I had my calls transferred to my cell from work while I was out. "This is Ms. Thomas." I said as I smiled at Keith. "Kaitlyn, I know you won't believe me, but this is your mother. Your real birth mother. You need to watch your back. Zavier isn't the guy who you think he is nor is Eric. They are playing you for a fool and are out to harm you." The strange woman said. "Hello? Who is this?" I quickly answered. "Is everything okay?" Keith asked as he saw how fast I went from smiling to frowning. "Ah, I'm not sure. Listen, I have to go." I informed Keith that I would call him later and apologized for cutting our lunch short.

I ran to the car and ordered my car to dial Zavier. I didn't get an answer. I continued to call him until he picked up. By the time I got to the law firm, I had dialed Zavier's number at least fifteen times. I was frustrated, but I really didn't have time to get all worked up and upset. "Carmen, are those files in my office and ready to go?" I asked as I was getting off the elevator. "Yes, Ms. Thomas." She replied. "Transfer only emergency phone calls and take a message for the others. I need to review these case files before the client comes in." I instructed her as I was still looking down at my phone trying to text Zavier. "Yes, Ms. Thomas." I entered my office trying to finish my text until I heard "Hello beautiful." Zavier said.

"What the hell are you doing here? Why are all these flowers here?" I said to him as I saw that my entire office was full of roses. "And, why weren't you answering your phone?" I said to him with frustration. "Baby...baby. Calm down. I was rushing to have all this ready, that I probably left my phone in the car. I wanted to surprise you and let the world know how much I love you." He replied apologetically and he kissed my forehead. I must say that I was happy that he wanted all the women to know that he was taken. "Oh, no not here. Remember what happened last time?" I asked Zavier as he got down on his knees. "Baby, I don't want any other woman. I love you and I want to spend the rest of my life with you. I promise that your every wish is my command. Will you make me the luckiest man on earth and be my wife?" He proposed and pulled out a big princess-cut diamond ring. Although that phone call was still in my mind, I still answered, yes. I decided not to bring it up and ruin what may be the best day of my life over something that may be nothing.

CHAPTER 11

Life was good for me. Over the course of months, Zavier had impressed me more and more each day. I can truly say that he wasn't the same man before and I was glad that we were finally gonna spend the rest of our lives together. I haven't talked to Keith since the last time I saw him and I felt like it was better this way. He didn't need to think that he had a chance nor did I want to have him hanging around like a lost puppy. However, Stan called and said that he was visiting since his team didn't go to the playoffs. I was glad to have my friend back around, but I didn't know how to tell him that I was engaged to Zavier.

"Cassandra?" I called out to my foster mother. "Yes, sweetheart?" She answered. Ugh, she thought we were the best of friends ever since I asked her to help with the wedding. "I want to add a cocktail hour while me and Zavier take pictures." I instructed as I looked at a menu of appetizers. "Sure, honey anything you want. It's your day." I noticed that she was kind of dry with her response so I asked her if she didn't think that was a good idea. "No, it's perfect. The groom is whom I questioning." She sighed. "See, this is why I didn't want to ask for your help because

I knew you couldn't stand the thought of me being happy." I said and slammed the book shut. "No baby. I want you to be happy. It's just that when you were with him last time he put you in that place and I don't want it to happen again." She remarked and rubbed my hair. "Nobody put me in that place, but me. It was nobody's fault, but mine. Okay!" I said to her as I moved her hand from my head. "So you plan to drain me dry I see." Eric observed as he walked in with Zavier. "You damn right." I said back to Eric. "Kait, baby that's not nice." Zavier said to me as he wrapped his arms around my waist and kissed me on the cheek. "So, you saying that I don't deserve it? So, I'm not good enough." I responded and pushed Zavier away. "Whoa. Whoa. Baby, calm down. That's not at all what I'm saying. I was just saying that maybe you can take it easy. It doesn't have to be a really big expensive wedding. As long as you're walking down the aisle, I could care less about what you're wearing or how much it cost." Zavier stated as he tried to pull me back to him. "So now I'm not worth it?" I said as I stormed out of the study. "Did I say something wrong?" Zavier asked Eric and Cassandra. "Welcome to the marriage life." Eric said to Zavier as he took a sip of his scotch. Cassandra politely excused herself to check on Kaitlyn without even glancing at Zavier.

Eric and Zavier made sure the coast was clear to talk before discussing business. "Now, all you have to do is stay with her until she turns thirty and the money is yours." Eric articulated as he closed the door and walked to his desk. "Fifty percent. Right?" Zavier noted as he poured himself a drink. "Hell naw.

You get twenty-five percent." Eric told him. "You said fifty percent and not twenty-five." Zavier said angrily. "Well, that was before your little girlfriend called and showed me what she had." Eric stated in reference to Carmen. "So as you can see, you are having to share your half with her. Let me ask you this question. Why in the hell would you get that hoe pregnant?" Eric wondered as he poured another shot of scotch. Zavier then filled him in on the entire story and what happened. Eric still called him a dumb ass and informed him that she promised to keep quiet just as long as she gets her cut. "How can you be sure she won't snitch?" Zavier asked. "Trust me, she has an opportunity of a life time and I doubt it that she would jeopardize it." Eric said. When the doors slid open, they were relieve to find Kaitlyn was on the phone so she didn't have a chance to hear what they said. "Okay, I'm on my way. Shut the hell up. Bye." Kaitlyn communicated into the receiver. "Baby, who where you talking to?" Zavier asked. "Stan. I gotta go pick him up at the airport." I told Zavier. "I thought he wasn't coming until this weekend?" He questioned. "Me too" I half-heartedly responded before I continued. "So listen, hold on to this and please let me tell him on my own time." I said and passed him the engagement ring. "If he is truly your friend, he'll be happy for you so just wear it." Zavier said to me as he was trying to put the ring back on my finger. "Baby, please. I don't ask for much okay. Just this once I need you to cooperate with me." I kissed him before I left. I saw the expression on his face wasn't a pleasant one, but he loved me and wanted me to be happy even if it meant not wearing my ring for a while.

As I got closer to the airport I couldn't help but to think when would be the best time to tell Stan that I was engaged. It has been months since we've seen each other because football season was in full effect, but we talked whenever he called. I wasn't sure if he ever gotten over his feelings that night we kissed and didn't want this to ruin our friendship again. But, I had to agree with Zavier that if Stan was truly my best friend, then he would be happy for me regardless of his feelings toward Zavier.

"Hey, gorgeous!" Stan said to me as he approached. "Stop." I replied as we hugged. "You look good. I'm mean you look aight." Stan said as he stood back and examined me from head to toe. "Whatever, bighead. Anyway, we're having a dinner at Cassandra and Eric's house. Would you like to come?" I offered. "Sure, as long as I can bring a guest?" Stan and motioned for someone to come over. "Stan, what have I told you about these THOT'S?" I said as I rubbed my forehead. "Heffa, who you calling a THOT?" Alivia said. "OMG! What are you doing here? And, of all people with him?" I remarked as we embraced. "Well, I ran into Stan a few weeks ago and he told me he was visiting, so here I am. But, never mind that. Where is it? Show me girl." Alivia screamed as she grabbed my hand. "Where is what?" Stan asked with a bewildered expression. I bucked my eyes at Alivia and hoped she would get the hint to not mention me being engaged and she did immediately. "Nothing, I was thinking about buying me another car that's all." I said to Stan in an effort he would believe me. "Well, Stan I will drop you off and come by and pick you around 7." I told him while we exited the airport. "My own personal chauffeur. Isn't that nice?" He smiled and hugged again. I was glad to have my two best friends there to share my happiness. I knew that Alivia was happy for me, but I wasn't sure how Stan would react. However, I knew I wanted to be the one to tell him and not to have him find out from anybody else. After I dropped Stan off, Alivia wanted to do a little shopping before the dinner. I didn't mind at all considering I haven't had a real "girl-friend" around to do those girly things with. "I'm sorry about earlier, Kait. I just thought that Stan already knew." Alivia apologized. "It's okay. No, I haven't told him yet. He can't stand Zavier." I told her as we were walked into a boutique. "For what it's worth, if he really loves and cares for you like I think he does, he won't be mad, he'll be happy." She declared to me. "I know deep down that he may be happy, but he still won't be pleased with my decision." I answered back. "Damn, I wish I had a man like that who was willing to go through hell and high water for me." We both laughed as she fanned herself. As we were on our way to the register, a familiar face sat at the counter. "Whoa, girl who is that fine piece of vanilla?" Alivia asked as she looked at Keith in admiration. "Hey Kaitlyn." He greeted me. Alivia cleared her throat to motion for me to introduce her to him. "Keith, this is my best friend, Alivia. Alivia, this is Keith. Now, goodbye." I immediately grabbed Alivia's arm to leave. "Wait, girl we didn't pay. Don't worry about it. I'm good for it and they know it. Let's go." I repeated and signaled for her to come on before Keith came out. "Kait, stop this." Keith begged as he ran towards me. "Um, I see this is my cue to leave. I'll wait for you by the car. Keith it was nice to meet you." Alivia dug the car keys from my purse. "Keith, I have nothing to say to you. I haven't accepted any of your phone calls or responded to your text. So that means that I don't wanna talk to you. Goodbye." I tried to walk away, but he took my arm and kissed me. Ah man, why did he have to do that? I forgot how much passion he had in his kiss. I quickly got myself together and pulled away, but not before I slapped him. "Don't you ever in your life put your hands on me again." I demanded while trying not to cry. "You're not sure if you wanna marry him. Are you?" Keith said as he tried to wipe my face. "Yes, I want to marry him. You don't know a damn thing about me." I yelled at him. "If you were so sure, then you would have blocked me from calling you and texting you. If you were sure, then you wouldn't have allowed me to kiss you that long. If you were sure, then you wouldn't be upset right now." He went on and on. "I'm upset because you just think that I am a piece of meat and belong to you." I knew what I just said didn't make any sense, but I had to say something. "I thought that we enjoyed our time together. What did I do wrong? Tell me so that I can fix it. I don't wanna lose you." He said as he rubbed my cheek. Honestly, I don't know what he did to have me not want to be around him. I did my best to think of something to say, but there was nothing. "I gotta go." I hurried away to my car to get away from him. I was praying that that he wouldn't chase after me. I knew that Keith was a temptation and in order to prevent myself from giving in to him, I would need to stay away from him.

On the way home I was dead silent. I couldn't explain what was going on and if it really was possible the reason why I ignored Keith, was due to my feelings for him. "Are we gonna talk about Keith or nah?" Alivia inquired as we pulled into the driveway. "Nah! And you didn't see him and did you meet him. Got it?" I scolded and pointed my finger. "Chill Kait. I am not that type of person and you know this." She replied and moved my finger from her face. Zavier came towards the car and I glanced in the mirror to make sure my makeup wasn't running because I didn't want him to think that anything was wrong. "Hey baby I missed you." Zavier said as he wrapped his arms around me and prepared to kiss me. I responded by wrapping my arms around his neck and told him the same. We were so caught up in each other arms, I forgot Alivia was there. "Hm...baby, wait." I mumbled as I tried to pull my lips from his. "You're right let's go to my house. The party doesn't start for another two hours." He noted. I laughed when I broke free to introduce the two. "Nice to finally meet you, Zavier. Aye, Kait I refuse to look at ya'll all night all lovey dovey. So, there's gonna be some men at this dinner, right?" She looked very uncomfortable at me. "No, just family." I laughed again. "Well, I might just be your in law soon." We both laughed as we walked towards the house. There was one thing for sure that if no one had a good time, Alivia made sure she did.

While I got dressed, I heard family members coming in downstairs asking my whereabouts. I had to be fantastic, after all it was my engagement party. I didn't tell Stan about it because I knew he wouldn't come. "Hey, I thought you had to pick Stan up?" Alivia asked as she helped me finish my hair. "I asked Eric to get him for me. I told him not to say anything and he won't. The only thing Eric likes to talk to Stan about is football." I saw that Alivia was staring off to space so I wasn't sure if she heard me or not. "Alivia? Alivia?" I called out as she had completely stopped helping me with my hair. "Sorry. It's just that....never mind." She said. "No, tell me. What is it? I hate when people start to say something then say never mind. If you wasn't gonna tell me, then you shouldn't have opened your mouth in the first place." I stated with an attitude. "Well damn, fine I'll tell you." She snapped her fingers. "Your dad?" She questioned. "Adoptive dad." I corrected her. "I've seen him before, but I don't know where?" She said. "Well, he is well known...so maybe that's why he looks familiar." I replied back because she was right, it wasn't nothing.

I finally made it to the dinner party and introduced my best friend Alivia to the family. She took a survey on who was single and who was taken before she started flirting. I told her who was who just in case things went down, even though everyone was basically my family. If a fight broke out, I am most definitely on Alivia's side. "Don't you know you're not supposed to wear white after Labor Day?" Stan examined my outfit and handed me a glass of wine. "Shut up and stop hating." I snatched the wine glass from him. "So, are you gonna tell me why we all dressed up? Wait, you own the law firm?" Stan said as he clicked his glass against mine. "No, not exactly." I commented as I took a sip of my wine. "Man, does he gotta be here?" Stan asked in a disgusted tone as he pointed to Zavier. "Uh, about that...we need to talk." I informed him as I tried to explain the situation, but before I could, I heard Zavier's voice. "May I have everyone's attention, please? Kaitlyn will you kindly join me by my side." Zavier commanded. . Oh my damn I uttered to myself as I walked away from Stan into Zavier's arms. "Kaitlyn, I want you to know that you have made me the happiness man on earth by saying yes." Zavier professed and slid the engagement ring back on my finger. I saw Stan's eyes fill with hatred as Zavier made his announcement that this was an engagement party. "Again, we thank all of you for celebrating this wonderful moment with us and in just three months, you will be looking at Mr. & Mrs. Zavier Price. Cheers!" Zavier said as he was closed his speech and raised his wine glass. Stan left the room and I knew that I had to go after him. "Where are you going?" Zavier said as he pulled me back. "I gotta find Stan and talk to him." I tried pulling away. "For what? You're acting like he's the one you're marrying." Zavier answered furiously. "Don't go there with me right now. Because as far as I'm concerned you gonna have me questioning if I really wanna marry you. Now, let me go." I ran outside to find Stan, but he was already half way up the street and I couldn't catch him. I knew that he was furious about the situation and I only wanted to tell him how sorry I was for not telling him sooner.

CHAPTER 12

I did the best I could in order to make sure that everyone else was enjoyed the party even though I didn't When I felt like I couldn't do it anymore, I politely excused myself from the room. "Are you okay?" Cassandra me when I told everyone I wasn't feeling well. "Yea, I'm just a little nauseous that's all." I replied and held my stomach. "I knew something was different about you." Cassandra mother consoled and rubbed my stomach. "Yes, I'm getting married." I told her and I tried hard to pull away from her grip. "No, I say in about seven months, we'll have a new member to the family." Everyone congratulated Zavier when Cassandra's mother expressed her suspicions. I paid her no attention and sauntered upstairs to my bedroom. I closed the door and laid across the bed wondering what Stan was doing. The look on his face hurt me more than him not actually being here. If looks could kill, I'd be six foot under right about now. "Come in." I answered to whomever knocked at the door. "So seven months?" Zavier said as he came in. "Unless she knows something I don't. Ain't nothing in this oven." I told him as he laid on the bed with me. "Why did you announce it like that?" I sat up. "Baby, he needed to know, and I would rather him hear it from me and hate me, then hear it from you and hate you. I know how much his friendship means to you and I didn't want you jeopardizing it." Zavier softly kissed my neck. "I know, but still you could have warned me." I mumbled as he kept kissing my neck. "I mean, you just...blurt...it out with....out....hmmm..." I moaned and tried to finish my sentence, but Zavier was making that very hard as he placed kisses on my neck and pushed his finger inside me. "Shh....come here." Zavier said as he was pulled me on top of his face. With every lick that I felt, I twitched. The way he was licking and slurping, you would have thought he was eating a Popsicle on a hot summer day. "Okay, baby. Stop." I said as I tried getting off his face. "Baby, thank you. I came, now stop." I moaned and tried to get off, but I felt him holding me even tighter. A part of me thought he enjoyed the idea of us getting caught because when he licked a certain spot, my moans became louder and louder and I had to place my hand over my mouth. And when he heard me doing that, he kept going at that same spot to make me moan even louder. "Baby, stop....." I moaned. "Not until I taste you cumming again." He mumbled licked me. It didn't take long for me to cum again as I grabbed his head to let him know that I reached orgasm "Do you feel better?" He asked. I shook my head yes and kissed him to taste what he found so fascinating. "I want you now!" I exclaimed and started unfastening the belt on his pants. He grabbed my hands and placed them behind my head and all I thought about was "yes, give it to me." Instead he told me that he wished he could but because he was on call that night to work the ER, he had to stop. "Baby, all I gotta do is tell Eric to make a phone call and you're off the hook." I pulled my hands away and attempted to reach in his pants. "I know that, but you know I take pride as a doctor and sex isn't on my mind right now." He stated as he got up. I was pissed off at him for getting me so horny and then just leaving. "How do you think it would make me feel if somebody died because I wasn't working that night?" He interrogated. I didn't respond to his question because I was still mad with him. "I promise you tomorrow morning, I'm gonna make love to you for hours. No matter how tired I am because I wanna please you." Zavier leaned in and kissed me, but I moved away. "I won't be here in the morning." I told him. "I forgot. Well, when I come home and see you naked in my bed…" Zavier said, but I interrupted him and made a note to him that I wasn't gonna be there, either. "What do you mean, baby?" He asked with a confused look. "Don't worry about it. Don't you gotta be at the hospital?" I retorted with an attitude. He kissed me on the forehead and told me that he loved me, but I didn't wanna hear it. All I could think about was how to get rid of being so horny without him.

Zavier called out to Eric to speak with him for a second outside. Eric knew what it concerned and didn't waste no time to meet him outside. "She wants me to come over?" Zavier told Eric. "Who?" Eric asked. "Carmen. She said that she needed to see me and after I told her no, she threatened us." Zavier rubbed his face. "Wait, she threaten you. I'm not the one who got the hoe pregnant. And besides I got other things to be more concerned about right now." Eric answered Zavier as he took a sip of his scotch. "Man, like what? I'm doing all of your dirty work for you. Your hands are washed and clean." Zavier said. "You know that girl that came with Stan?" Eric asked. "Yeah, I think her name is Lisa?" Zavier asked. "No, it's Alivia and I think she knows about me." Eric informed Zavier. Zavier didn't say anything because he was still trying to figure out why Eric would be so concerned about Alivia. "Would you like to elaborate?" Zavier motioned with his hands. "To make a very long story short. Your fiancée, my adopted daughter, is really my niece." Eric said as he took another sip. Zavier was dumb founded when he heard this. "Time out! Time out! Your niece? How did that happen? I mean I know how, but I mean she was in foster care." He was totally confused. Eric was silent because he was still trying to figure what to do if Alivia recognized him and it got out. "So, are you gonna tell me or what?" Zavier asked. "Don't worry about this. Aight! I got this. You just go over there and handle that bitch before I will." Eric instructed Zavier as he went back into the house. Zavier did as he was told and was heading over to Carmen's house. However, he was trying to put what Eric just said in perspective and how he could use it against Eric in case he tried to double cross him.

    I didn't think that Stan would get that upset about me marrying Zavier. I knew that he wouldn't be thrilled at the thought about it, but at the same time I figured if he saw how happy I was, he would be happy for me too. "Can I come in?" Alivia was at the bedroom door. "It's open." I said. "Are you okay?" She probed with concern. I told her that I was, but she could see right through me and told me that I wasn't. "So what are you gonna do?" She asked another question. "Get married." I said as I got and straightened my hair. "Is this truly what you want to do?" Again, she asked a question. "What is up with all the quizzing? If we gonna play twenty-one question let me get a drink first." I replied with an attitude. "Look, I'm not trying to make you feel any worse right now. All I'm saying is, I just hope that you're not rushing into anything that you don't really want." She restated. "What? Don't I look happy? I'm happy. Zavier is wonderful to me. He gives me anything I want and he is caring, sweet, and kind and..." I paused for a moment and tried to think of more things to say about Zavier. When I stopped I saw that Alivia was giving me a very nonchalant look. I asked her what that look was for and she just said nothing. "No, say it. We've always been honest with each other in the past so no need to hold back now." I confronted her. "You really want the truth?" She was getting on my nerves as I told her to spill it already. "After I saw you today with Zavier and Keith, I can tell that you care more for Keith then you do for Zavier." She implied. "What the hell are you talking about? You don't even know what is going on with me and Keith so how can you even fix your mouth to say that? Plus, you just told me that I had a thing for Stan a few months ago. I wish you make up your damn mind about who I love." I yelled at her rudely. "See what you just said? If there was nothing going on, for number one you wouldn't be this upset, and number two, you would have used past terms. And number three, you wouldn't even be having this conversation with me if you were one hundred percent sure about Zavier." Alivia pointed out to me. I said nothing as I left Alivia in the room by herself. I was so overwhelmed with everything that was going on that I just left. I didn't know where I was going nor did I care, I just wanted out.

As I was driving I realized my thought took me to Stan's house. I hoped he was home and that maybe we could possibly talk. I stood there for a few moments after ringing the doorbell just to give him a chance to answer, but he didn't so I got back in my car and decided to give him a call. At first there wasn't an answer and then my phone beeped to let me know I had a text message. I thought it was Stan, but it was Zavier letting me know that he was going to be later than he thought at work and he didn't want me to be alone at home that long and told me the wanted me to spend the night at my folks house. I really didn't care because my mind wasn't on dealing with them at the moment. My focus was trying to talk to Stan. We've had plenty of fights and arguments, but I've never seen him that upset before.

I left Stan's house and headed to the strip mall and sat in the parking lot to gather my thoughts. However, I realized whenever I was having a bad day that Stan was the one who I talked to all the time and he wasn't there and Zavier wasn't either. It just crossed my mind that I was alone for the first time without anyone to comfort me when I needed it the most; I didn't know what to do. I couldn't breathe, I couldn't catch my break, and I was scared to be alone. As my emotions became stronger, I texted Keith a 911 emergency message asking him to meet me in the parking lot where we first met. I had promised myself to stay away from him, but I needed him. I sat there and tried to calm down, but different thoughts raced across my head. I kept thinking what if me and Stan never spoke again, or what if I never see him again? The thoughts made it worse and worse and I didn't know how to stop thinking like that. I heard a tap on my window as I turned my head to look I saw that it was Keith. I immediately opened the door and flew into his arms, panting. "Shh...it's okay. Calm down, Kait. I'm here, breathe for me. In through your nose and out of your mouth." Keith coached as he held me close to his chest and rubbed my back. I tried it and I could feel myself slowly calming down. "I don't wanna be here." I lamented to Keith as I was still trying to catch my breath. "Okay, okay. Where do you wanna go?" He asked as he wiped my face. "With you." I said as I looked up at him. He asked me if I was sure and I nodded my head, yes. I knew that I would be safe with Keith because he never made me feel uncomfortable whenever we were around each other.

As we got to his house, I saw that he had a barn sitting down by the side of the house. I asked if he was a Texas Chainsaw Massacre killer. He laughed a little and replied, no. It felt good to laugh instead of crying, but I realized that I was talking to Keith and not Stan. I didn't mind talking to Keith it was just the fact that I've always talked to Stan every time I was going through something. Keith saw my eyes watering up again as we walked in his house. He sat me down on the couch and told me he would be right back. I laid my head on the pillow end of the couch and balled up like a baby as tears fell down my face. "Here Kait, drink this." Keith handed me a bottle of water. I took it from him and swallowed a few sips to see if it would help. "Do you feel better?" Keith asked. I shook my head no and he just began to rub my back again. That was the moment that I realized he hadn't asked me what was wrong yet and I knew that he was just giving me time. He was being understanding, caring, and compassionate, and that's when I knew I had to have him.

I turned to Keith and positioned my body on his lap. I felt him wrap his arms around me as he kissed me back. I whispered in his ear and began to unbutton his shirt. He looked at me with his blue eyes as he laid me on the couch, but got up quickly. "What are you doing?" Keith moved away. "You don't wanna do this." He said. "Yes, I do." I responded as I got up to kiss him some more. He pushed me back and begged me to sit down. "What the hell is wrong with you?" I asked Keith as I refused to sit down. "Look, any man would have taken advantage of you and your vulnerability, but I'm not that kind of man. I can see that your emotions are making you do things that you really don't want to do and you're going to regret it once you come back to reality." He backed up as he made sure to keep distance between us. "I don't wanna feel this. This hurt, I don't wanna feel it. I want anything, but this. So please, just do this for me okay?" I begged Keith as I was still trying to kiss him. "No, Kait, I'm not going to do this. I want you. Believe me I truly do, but not like this. I want to make love to you and not just have sex with you." He wiped more tears away. I sat down hating the fact that I wasn't going to get what I wanted, but I loved the fact that Keith was being respectful and strong when I couldn't. He asked me if it was okay if he held me and I complied. I guess sometimes you really do just need someone to hold you until you fall asleep.

I wasn't sure what time it was, but I do know that when I opened my eyes I noticed that Keith was still holding me. It felt so good to be held and especially by Keith. Wait! What am I saying? I shouldn't be here like this with him. "Good morning." He laid a kiss on my forehead. "Ugh, good morning." I replied dryly. "Would you like breakfast? I make a mean omelet." He declared "That sounds good, but I'm pretty sure my fiancée is wondering where I am." I blurted out. "So it is true?" He asked very nonchalantly. "Listen, thanks for everything and I really do mean that." I told him as he walked me to the door. He then asked if it was okay to give me a hug and I didn't mind hugging him at all. As I was rushing out the door, I realized that Keith had asked for confirmation that me and Zavier where in fact engaged. I didn't answer because I knew that would of lead into more questions and I was ready to deal with it. I wanted us to end on a good note, plus, I appreciated the fact that he was a gentleman and a friend.

My heart was racing as I saw how many missed phone calls was on my phone from Zavier, but there were no missed phone calls from Stan. I wasn't sure what I was going to say to Zavier and how to explain to him why I missed his phone calls. I decided to figure all of that out later as I dialed Stan's phone before reaching Zavier's house. "Hello?" Stan answered. "What? No, sarcasm this time? Usually..." I tried to continue, but Stan was very blunt that he was busy and asked what I wanted. "Well, can we meet for lunch and talk?" I asked. "That's impossible." He said to me. "Look, I know you don't like Zavier, but he has changed." I tried to convince Stan. "No, I'm saying it's impossible because I'm back in L.A." He informed me. I couldn't believe that my actions made him so upset that he flew all the way back home without saying goodbye. As I pulled into the driveway, I tried my best to get Stan to talk to me more, but he made his words short and simple. "Well, can I call you later?" I asked as I saw Zavier open the door. "Whatever." He abruptly ended the call. I couldn't understand why he was so upset with me marrying Zavier. I knew that he didn't really care for him, but just for him to act like he didn't care about me was out of the ordinary.

"Where the hell have you been?" Zavier angrily asked as he opened my car door. I didn't respond because I was thinking if I should tell him the truth or lie about it. I didn't want to lie, but I couldn't tell him the truth even though nothing happened. "I had to get out that house." I told him as we walked towards the house. "And go where?" He quizzed again. Again, I was thinking of telling the truth, but I just couldn't.

"I was on the strip." I told him and threw myself on the couch. "By yourself?" He kept the questions going one after another. Damn, why is he interrogating me? The last time I checked I was the lawyer and he was the doctor. "Yes, I just needed some time to think and when I got tired, I got a room at the hotel." He placed my feet on his lap to massage them. "That doesn't make sense to me. You could have come here while I was at work or stayed at the hotel with Lisa." He said. "It may have not made sense to you, but it made sense to me. I needed to be alone, okay. Please, can we talk about this later?" I was tired of his questions and pulled my feet away from him. "Sure." He answered. I then asked him who was Lisa, and he told him the girl who came with Stan. I corrected him by telling him her name was actually Alivia. I don't know how he got Lisa out of Alivia. "Baby, don't ever do that again. I don't know what I would do if anything happened to you." He cautioned. I could tell that he was truly concerned for me and that's when I knew how much I loved him. "I love you." I said to him as I sat up to kiss him. "I love you too baby." He said back.

As I kissed him, I placed my hands in his pants. I was getting horny as I started thinking about what we didn't finish from last night and what I wanted to start with Keith. I felt him trying to lay me back down on the sofa, but instead I pushed him back and got on my knees. This was something I never done before, but I was feeling so freaky with all the different thoughts running through my head that it made me want to do it. "Baby, what are you doing?" He asked because he knew that I've never done it before.

I didn't reply as I pulled it out to lick the head. He started to moan as I started to place my lips around the head. I didn't know what I was doing, but I imagine that it wasn't that hard to figure out. "Damn, baby that feels so good." He said as he rested his head on the sofa. I grabbed it with one hand as I tried to push more of him in my mouth, but it just kept growing and I couldn't. I must've been doing a good job with all of the slurping and spit running down that he pushed me back off of it and laid me down on the floor to return the favor. I grabbed his head as he placed his finger inside of me while licking at the same time. He didn't do it long this time because we both wanted each other too badly. I wrapped my arms around his neck as he stroked up and down. "Ah, baby yes that feels so good." I said as he was kissing me on my neck. "You feel...." He said as he stopped. "Why you stop?" I asked him as he interrupting my orgasm "I thought I heard something." He said as he turned his head to the door. "It's probably nothing, baby." I ensured him. We continued to make love, but before the both of us could cum, we heard a loud boom outside as if a bomb had went off. Zavier jumped up and ran to the window. "What the hell!" He yelled as he grabbed his boxers to go outside. I was afraid to go see what it was, so I just grabbed the blanket and waited for him to come back inside. "What's going on?" I asked him as he ran to get his phone. He didn't answer, but for some reason I heard him call 911. I decided to see what was going on with the blanket still wrapped around me. When I walked to the door I saw that my car was on fire and pieces of it were everywhere. I couldn't comprehend at the moment what was going on so I walked closer to my car. "Baby, get in the house." Zavier pleaded as he pulled me back in the house. "The police and fire department are on their way." He told me, but I still couldn't comprehend. "I gotta go." I said as I started throwing my clothes back on. "Go where? You're safe here." He wrapped me in his arms with embrace. "Don't touch me!" I screamed. "What's wrong?" He asked. I just kept pacing back and forth talking. "I gotta leave. He's coming. He's going to get me. But, I won't let him this time. I'm gonna be ready for him. He won't see it coming. I wasn't ready last time, but I'm ready." I kept saying to myself as I walked to the window and paced back and forth. "Baby, come here. Baby no one is going to get you. I'm here." Zavier said. I felt hands touching me and I just started throwing my hands everywhere. "Help! Help! Somebody help me!" I screamed out. "Kaitlyn! Kaitlyn! Baby stop. It's me. Open your eyes and look at me. Look at me baby." Zavier yelled at her in hopes of getting her back to reality. He was relieved when he realized she had stopped as she had worked herself into a frenzy, but as he got closer he slowly realized the reason; Kaitlyn had passed out.

CHAPTER 13

I heard a lot of commotion going on as I opened my eyes, and for some reason I felt really exhausted. I turned my head to see that the police and fire department was at the door. "Baby, what's going on?" I muttered to Zavier. "Ma'am, do you have any enemies or know anybody who might want to hurt you?" I was silent. "No, she doesn't. It might have just been some kids." Zavier answered the police. "Sir, kids would set poop on fire on your porch. They wouldn't blow up a whole car, matter of fact they would just steal the car." The police stated. "Well, actually I got attacked a few months back and then I got a weird phone call." I told the officer. "Phone call?" Zavier questioned. "Yeah, a really strange phone call about you and Eric." I said as I looked at Zavier. "Did you recognize the number or the voice?" The officer asked me. "Uh, no the number was blocked, but it was a woman and she said that she was my birth mother." I replied. "Okay, well we got your information and if we run across anything we'll give you a call. Until then, ma'am, we suggest you never go anywhere alone and get security lights and a good alarm system." He commented before he left.

I went upstairs to take a bathe as Zavier made sure that everything was locked. "Kaitlyn?" Zavier called out. I heard him, but I was too tired to respond. "Kaitlyn?" He called out again as he walked into the bathroom as I started to run the water. "Yes, baby." I weakly replied. "What phone call and when did you get it?" He asked. "Ugh, a few months back. Whew, why am I so tired?" I said as I yawned. "You had an episode. But, back to this phone call." He interrupted. "An episode? Please don't tell Eric baby. I do not want to go back to the crazy house." I begged of him. He said okay, but still wanted to know about the phone call. I told him that it was nothing and that it was just someone playing on the phone telling me that he was a bad guy and this and that. "Baby, it was probably Cassandra." I said. He looked at me strange when I said that, but then I explained that she really didn't care for him. He shrugged his shoulders and told me that he was going back downstairs to check things out. I was glad because that bath was calling my name.

Zavier made sure he closed the door to the bedroom so that he could hear Kaitlyn when she came out. He knew that there was only one person who did this and that was Carmen. "You are pushing it." Zavier said as Carmen answered the phone. "Now, you know that I mean business. We are your family." She stated as she was referring to her and the baby that she was carrying. "I know that. Once I'm done with her, we can be a family like I promised." He assured her. "She belongs back in the nut house the way she was prancing back and forth talking to herself." She responded with a deep laugh. "Wait, what? You were here watching?" He asked her. "I sure was. I saw everything." She stated. "Enough, enough. Stop with the weird phone calls to her and don't blow anything else up." He requested of her. Carmen was confused when he said phone call. "I admitted that I blew the bitch car up, but I've never called her. Don't get me wrong I've thought about it, but I can't stand the fact that I have to pretend to like her at work so why call." She told him. He quickly told Carmen to back off and to not bother Kaitlyn again as he heard the upper bedroom door open. "Where you going baby?" Zavier asked as he saw I was dressed. "I just need to get out the house for a while baby." I told him. "Well, take the truck sweetheart and call me if you need anything." He said as he kissed me. I told him that I would be okay and not to worry, but I knew that he was just being concerned for my safety.

I decided to meet with Alivia for breakfast even though I was still mad at her. But, I would have to admit that she was partially right about me and Keith. I did have some feelings for him, but I was in love with Zavier. "Are you still mad at me?" Alivia asked as I sat down. "Of course not. After all you're the only friend I have left right now." I told her. "Well, gee thanks. I feel so special." She responded sarcastically. "I didn't mean it like that. I meant that you're the only friend that knows me and really care." I responded. She asked what happened to Stan and I told her that he went back home. "Seriously? He flew all the way back to California because you're marrying Zavier?" "Yep. I never thought in a million years that we would ever stop being friends. We've fussed with each other before, but within fifteen minutes we're over it." I told her and she had a smug look on her face. "What is that look for?" I asked her. "Damn, girl. You got all the men. I need you to teach me a few things so I could get like you." She said as she took a sip of water. "I only have one man and his name is Keith." Before I knew it I had placed Keith's name where Zavier's should have been. Alivia almost spit out her water as she got choked when she heard me say Keith's name. "Uh, honey what happened to Zavier?" She asked as I looked away hoping that she wouldn't have caught my mistake. "I meant to say Zavier. So are you ready to order? I'm hungry." I hoped she would drop the subject at hand. "No ma'am. We not gonna act like that didn't just happen, especially the way you jumped down my throat last night. Speaking of last night. Is that who you were with?" She grilled me down as she kept asking me who I was with last night. I tried to ignore her, but she just got louder. "Lower your voice." I mouthed to her as people started looking at her. "Well then tell me. Damn, I mean you act like we just met." She said with an attitude. "Heffa, we did just meet like a few months ago." I replied back smartly. "You know what. I see why Stan left. If we are supposed to be your friends, then you should be able to tell us everything. No matter if it is good or bad or if we'll like it or not. Friends don't lie to friends. I tell you what, when you feel like being a friend give me a call." She said and got up to leave. I couldn't understand what was going on with my two best friends and why they hated me so. Is it really that deep if I don't tell them everything that goes on in my life? I felt like some things should be kept private especially when it comes to my childhood. I didn't sleep worth crap last night considering the fact I was still dealing with my issues with Alivia and Stan. Going to work was the last thing I felt like doing, but I knew that it would keep my mind busy. I heard someone knocking at my door and I figure if I ignored them then they would leave because I didn't have the energy to deal with any "BS" today. "Are you okay?" Zavier asked as he walked in. I was excited to see him because he had been working all weekend. I quickly got up and ran into his arms and started crying. "Hey. Hey. Baby what's wrong?" He asked. I told him nothing and requested that he hold me as tight. He did what I requested and asked me what was wrong again. "Nothing baby. It's just planning this wedding has got me stressed and on edge that's all." I lied. "And see this is why I wanted a small wedding with just you and me. Because of this right here." He reminded me as he planted kisses on my lips. "I know baby. But, I've always wanted a big wedding and you know this." I commented and wiped my face. "I tell you what. Let me get some rest because I just got off and when you come home, I promise whatever you want it's granted." He promised and winked his eye. I started telling him the things I expected to see when I got home and he just shook his head in agreement. It felt good to feel appreciated and wanted by the man I loved. "I promise you when you come home you gonna get all of that and more." He started kissing me again. I knew he was referring to sex when he said more considering the fact I only asked for dinner, a hot bubble bath and a full body massage. "Okay. Okay. Stop baby, I gotta get back to work." I said as I was shoved him away because of how I've been feeling I was starting to get a little horny and sex in the workplace wasn't an option at the moment. "I'll be waiting on you my queen." He said as he kissed my hand. Zavier has been nothing, but wonderful and that's why it was hard for me to understand why Stan still disliked him.

As Zavier walked towards the elevator he saw that Carmen had an evil glare in her eye. He heard Kaitlyn paging Carmen instructing her to sign for a package at the front desk. She quickly got up in order to jump at the opportunity of being alone with Zavier. "So what's wrong with the bitch now?" Carmen asked after the elevator doors closed. "Don't start with me about this right now. I'm not in the mood." Zavier reprimanded. "Fine. Whoa!" Carmen said as she grab her belly. "What's wrong?" Zavier asked. "Nothing the baby just kicked. Wanna feel?" Carmen asked him. He smiled and reached to rub her belly not realizing that the elevator had reached its designation. "I hope this is your sister." Stan said as the elevator doors had opened and he saw Zavier holding and rubbing Carmen's belly. "What the hell are you doing here? Kaitlyn told me you left." Zavier asked Stan. "You didn't answer my question, and yeah I did leave, but you know what I couldn't let a bastard like you ruin my best friends life." Stan remarked as Zavier exited the elevator to get in his face. "You really do love her don't you? You are pathetic. She doesn't love you like that man and besides all the good loving I've been giving her and the way she's been saying my name. I'm surprise she still remembers you." Zavier replied with a smirk on his face. "Aye, man you need to get your ass out of my face or do you want me to tell her what's going on between you and Carmen." Stan said as he took a step back in order not to hit Zavier. "Wait a minute. How do you know her name playa?" Zavier asked Stan. "Zavier, look at this." Carmen demanded and shoved a brown envelope to him. "Not now." He told her. "Dammit, look." She said again as she handed him a picture out of the envelope. As he looked down, he saw that it was a picture of him and Carmen sleeping together at his home. "You really don't like me do you?" Zavier asked Stan. "I don't know what you're talking about man." Stan said as he bumped into Zavier to get on the elevator. "You sneaky bastard. This ain't over playa by a long shot." Zavier threatened Stan. "Do you think he really did this?" Carmen asked. "C'mon you can't be that stupid. Who else did this? He's in love with her and hates the fact that he can't have her. So, desperation cause for desperate measures." Zavier answered her rhetorical question as he reached for the entire envelope of pictures. "So what now?" She asked. Zavier told her not to worry and that he was going to take care of the situation at hand. His phone rang, so he told Carmen to head back upstairs in case it was Kaitlyn. But, when he saw who it was he was relieved. "Hey, I'm glad you called because we got another problem." Zavier updated Eric. He knew that Eric was the go to guy for problem solving and that it was gonna get handled.

I kept watching the clock to make sure that I wasn't late for my meeting at twelve, but when I looked at the clock and saw that it was after one I decided to call the client. "Hi, um did you forget that we had a meeting at twelve today?" My client then begin to tell me that they decided to choose another lawyer because I was too expensive. I hung up the phone after that because I'm expensive for a reason and that's because I always win. "Come in." I said as I heard a knock at the door. I was stunned to find Stan walking into my office. "Sorry are you busy?" He asked me. "No, no. I was just finishing up a phone call. How did? I mean, what did? Who?" I was stumbling over my words trying to understand what has happened in order for him to just show up after the last time we saw each other. "First, let me apologize for how I acted at your engagement party, but you could have told me that you were engaged to Zavier. I was more upset at the fact that you felt like you couldn't talk to me." He plopped down in the chair in front of my desk. "I know I should have told you, but I knew that you would have been mad at me for giving Zavier another chance." I told him as tears formed in my eyes. Stan immediately got up and came around my desk to hold me. I've missed his hugs so much and it felt good to know that he still cared. "I wasn't trying to get you upset. I just thought that after everything we've been through that we could always tell each other anything." He said and cleaned the tears away from my face. Stan had made me realized how important our friendship was and that he would always be there for me no matter what. "Stan, I have

something else to tell you." I said as we walked over
to the couch in my office. "You don't have to say it.
I know already." He said. "Wait, how could you know
this? Nobody knows because I've never told anybody."
I said to him with a confused look. "Listen, I just knew
that it was a matter of time. I only ask that you call
me when it's time." He said as he pointed his finger at me. I was really confused at this moment as
I was listened to Stan. Then it dawned on me that
he thought that I was pregnant. "Whoa. Stan you
know me better than that." I told him. "So, you're not
pregnant?" He asked. I told him that I wasn't as we
laughed at the thought of me being pregnant. Because we both know that I love my figure, besides, I
don't do well with pain.

After the good laughed we shared, Stan inquired
about what I needed to tell him. I almost didn't want
to tell him because I was enjoying our friendship getting back to normal. "Well, what I wanted to tell you
was...?" I paused as a tear rolled down my face. Stan
told me that whatever it was he promised that he
wasn't going to be mad. "Remember when you asked
why I got sent to the mental institution?" I asked him
and he nodded his head, yes. "Well, my breakdown
was only half of it. Yes, me catching Zavier cheating upset me, but really that was only a small part." I
said to him as I hesitated from telling him the truth.
I didn't want him to be disgusted with me. "It's okay
Kait. I'm not gonna be mad." He told me as he rubbed
my back. "Well, do you remember how after college
you always made fun of me for being a virgin?" I
asked. "Yeah?" He said with a puzzled look. "I was a

virgin because I was scared." I told him as I looked away. He told me to stop looking everywhere and focus on just him. I was trying too, but it was hard. "Stan, I was....um.... touched. And I don't mean in a good way and not at an appropriate age." I had finally let out. "Wait, Kait? Are you trying to tell me that you were molested as a child?" He asked as he reached for my hand. I nodded my head yes as I was crying. "I mean, but by who. You told me that your foster mother wasn't married." He said with a pause as he got up. I tried to cover up the fact that it was Eric, but Stan knew that I was adopted straight from foster care into Eric's and Cassandra's care. "Does Cassandra know about this?" He was angry. I told him that I wasn't for sure if she did or didn't. "That son of a bitch. I'm gonna kill him." Stan sprinted to the door. "Stan! No! Don't say anything. Please! Just let it go." I pleaded with him as he ran out of my office. Everyone stared at me as I kept yelling for Stan to stop. "What the hell are you looking at?" I asked everyone as I walked back towards my office and slammed the door. The look in Stan's eyes meant business and I knew that he meant what he said. I had to stop him because I was afraid that he would be successful and I couldn't lose him, especially over a bastard like Eric.

CHAPTER 14

A million things flooded my head as I was on my way to Eric's house. I was praying that Stan hadn't gotten there yet and if he did that he hasn't done something he would regret. "Hello?" I answered. "Hey babe. I've been trying to reach you all day." Zavier said. "Listen, right now isn't a good time can I call you back later?" I responded. "Sure. But, what's wrong? You don't sound like yourself." He asked. I promised him that I would explain everything to him later on that night as I hung up the phone. It wasn't that I was trying to keep Zavier in the dark, but my main focus was Stan and I wouldn't forgive myself if he ruined his life for me.

As I parked my car in the driveway, I heard a lot of yelling and I feared for the worse. My heart was beating fast and I could barely catch my breath as I ran towards the door. I saw that glass was broken everywhere and furniture misplaced when I stepped in the doorway. They were still yelling and tussling with each other as I stumbled over some stuff in the kitchen. "Stan stop it." I screamed as I tried to pull him off Eric but considering the fact that he was a football player it was very difficult for me to do. "I'm going to kill you, you son of bitch." Stan said as he strangled Eric. "What is going on in here?" Cassandra said as she walked in with her hands full of grocery bags. "I'm pressing charges. You are all my witnesses. You saw that he attacked me for no reason." Eric said as he wiped the blood from his nose. "If anyone should be pressing charges it's Kait. How could you do that to her? You bastard?" Stan said as he tried to reach for Eric, but I wouldn't let him get close. "Will someone please enlighten me on what the hell is going on?" Cassandra demanded. The room was dead silent as Stan's eyes glared at me. I didn't open my mouth but instead attempted to flee the room, but Stan stopped me. I gave him the look of fear begging him not to make me do this, but he insisted that it had to be done. "Will someone explain to me what the hell is going on right now or I'm calling the police?" Cassandra "Good. Call the Police, Mrs. Thomas." Stan stated to Cassandra. "Excuse me, Stanley? So, do you wanna go to jail?" "Oh, no. I won't be the one going. On the other hand your husband will be." He informed her. "What the hell are you talking about? You broke into my house and assaulted me." Eric said "Well, you're right and wrong there. I knocked and asked could I come in and you said yes, and then after the invite, I whooped your ass?" Stan shouted at Eric. After listening to them going back and forth, I just couldn't take it anymore. "Enough! Enough! Stop! Just stop! Eric, stop the lies okay. Stop lying about all those years of sneaking into my room late nights acting like nothing happened and don't stand there as if you don't know what I'm talking about. I can still remember it like yesterday with the smell of scotch on your breath and on my pajamas. And Cassandra, don't even look so surprised and act like you never knew this because you did." I cried loud with tears flooding my face. "Kaitlyn, I swear I had no idea he was doing that to you. I promise you." Cassandra tried to comfort me, but I wouldn't let her. "You sick bastard. She's your flesh and blood how could you do that? Something is really wrong with you. I wished I would have known because I would have had your ass thrown in jail." Cassandra spewed her words out to Eric, but right after she did he slapped her. Stan immediately sucker punched Eric for hitting Cassandra. "Flesh and blood? I'm not understanding. I'm adopted that doesn't makes us related at all except for having the same last name." I stated to Cassandra. "Kaitlyn, sweetie, it means that not only are you related by name, but you are related by blood." She said as she grabbed my hand. I told her I didn't understand. "Eric is your uncle, honey." She said without batting an eye. I looked at him with even more hatred. I didn't want to know the reason why or how could he do that to me now that I knew the truth about us. I only wanted to get out of there as soon as possible.

I could still hear Eric saying something about pressing charges when we left, but Stan wasn't concerned about that. He saw the look on my face after I heard the news and knew that I wasn't taking it too well. I only wanted to leave. "Kait, are you okay?" He asked. I didn't answer and he knew that I wasn't. "Where do you wanna go?" I didn't wanna go home right then because I wasn't ready to face Zavier. "Do you mind if we sit at your house for a while?" I wondered aloud. He said he didn't mind and was glad he kept his house, otherwise, we would be in a hotel and he wouldn't be responsible for whatever happened next. I could tell that he was trying to make me laugh, but this time it wasn't working. My emotions were all confused and I didn't know how to feel. I wanted to be angry for what Eric did to me all those years, and I wanted to cry because I didn't understand how he could do that to me now that I just found out we were related. There were so many unanswered questions and I wanted to know the truth to everything. My phone buzzed and I knew Zavier was going to be upset with me later because I kept rejecting his calls. But, I knew that once I told him what was going on that he would understand. "Don't you wanna call him back?" Stan asked me as we pulled in front of his old house. "No, I don't feel like talking right now. I just wanna lay down and forget this ever happened." I replied and headed heading to the guest room. "Kait, you need to talk about it or it's gonna make you feel worse." He told me. I didn't respond as I kept walking up the stairs even after he called my name again. I didn't want to talk. I only wanted to be left alone and for this pain of deceit to disappear.

I went downstairs to get me a shot of tequila because I couldn't sleep and figured if I got tipsy enough then maybe I could get a little rest. As I was making my way down I started to hear someone talking. "Stan, are you done here?" I said as I turned the corner to the kitchen. "Come here." I heard a man's voice say that didn't sound nothing like Stan's. When I was finally in the kitchen doorway I saw that it was Eric and he was talking to a little girl who looked exactly like me. I tried to go in, but something blocked me. "I won't hurt you I promise." He told the little girl. "Run! Run! Run!" I kept shouting to the little girl as she was now backed into a corner. "It won't hurt this time, I promise. You might even like it. I only want to help you grow into a beautiful young lady." Eric said as he picked the little girl up in his arms. She looked at me with fear as he took her downstairs into the basement. "Fight him. Do something, anything." I was yelling as I was still unable to go into kitchen as if there was an invisible barrier. I ran all through the house trying to find a way in or something to break the barrier, but it was useless. Leaving to go get help sounds like the only way possible, but before I could get to the front door I felt something run down my leg. When I glanced down I saw that it was blood. "Why didn't you help me?" I heard a tiny voice say. As I turned around I saw the little girl with blood running down her pajamas. "I told you to run and to fight. You let him do this to us. You're pathetic and disgusting. I hate you! I hate you!" I kept telling her over and over. Then there was a flash of light and the little girl disappeared and I was there alone until I heard my name being called. I knew it was Eric and I wasn't going to let him touch me. "There's my girl." He slurred with a strong smell of scotch on his breath. "You're not going to touch me again you bastard." I told him as I pushed him away and starting hitting him. "Stop. Stop." He kept repeating. "Now, you want me to stop? I've asked you to stop over and over again and you never did. You stole my life. You stole my childhood." I told him as I stood up and started kicking him. "Kaitlyn, please stop. Stop! Stop, it's me." Stan said. I had realized that I was dreaming and Stan was there trying to wake me up. "It hurts Stan. Why? Why me? What did I do to deserve this?" I screamed out as I was crying. "Nothing, Kait. You didn't do anything wrong. It's not your fault, okay?" He said as he pulled me close to him to comfort me. I heard the doorbell rang just in time, and I wished that it wasn't Cassandra. I didn't have the strength to deal with her right now. "It's probably Alivia. I called her last night to see if she could come over. I knew you wouldn't mind seeing her." He said as he kissed my forehead before going downstairs to get the door. He was right I didn't mind seeing Alivia and even though we may not agree on everything I knew that in my time of need she would be there. "Kaitlyn, can you come down please?" Stan yelled out. It was only proper for us to sit downstairs and discuss the matters at hand. I just hoped that they would be able to help me get through this. "I know that it's early, but I really need a shot right about now." I said with a chuckle as I entered the den. "Are you okay?" Zavier rushed to hug me. "I'm fine, but what are you doing here?" I asked him. "Well, after I couldn't reach you I went by your parent's house and the house was a mess. Eric told me where to find you. Are you okay? What happened?" He asked me. "Did he say anything else?" I asked Zavier. "No. Baby can you please tell me what's going on? You don't look like you're okay. What did you do?" Zavier questioned Stan as he walked in his direction. "Me? Are you serious right now? I should be asking....." Stan paused because he could see how it was upsetting me.

As Stan left to go get the door, Zavier walked toward me to hold me because he could see that I had so much pain in my eyes. Zavier kept repeating the same questions over and over, but I just didn't want to repeat myself so I waited until everyone was in the room. "Will you answer me baby?" Zavier asked. I looked at him with tears as he was rubbed my face as I could tell he was hurt that I wouldn't talk. "Stan, if that's Alivia you guys can come in here." I shouted out. Alivia entered before Stan unsure of what was about to happen. I asked if everyone would take a seat because I only wanted to say this once. Zavier refused to sit because he wanted to know what was going on, but I assured him that he was about to find out in just a second.

"Stan, you already know the situation at hand so this isn't new to you." I started off with a deep breath. A pause kept coming along as I kept trying to get Eric's name out of my mouth. Just the thought of him made me angry and my flesh crawl. "I just found out that Eric is my uncle, and not only that, he molested me as child. So, now do you see why I hate him with a passion?" I said amidst tears. . Zavier quickly came to my side to hold me and told me that it was okay. I told him that it wasn't okay and that Eric ruined my life. Stan kept telling me that it wasn't over and that he was gonna finish what he started. Everyone had a comment, but Alivia. I peeped over Zavier's shoulder and Alivia didn't seem to be bothered. "What is it?" I asked her. She said it was nothing, but her facial expressions gave her away every time. "Don't say it's nothing when it is. I know that look." I told her as I tried to calm myself down. "I don't want you to be mad." She cautioned. I instructed her to tell me what it was and how it was impossible for me to be mad at the moment. "Well, after you left the night of your engagement party, I was still trying to figure out where I've seen Eric before. So, as I was leaving I asked Eric if I could speak with him outside and he agreed. When we got outside, he asked if you were okay because he saw you crying on your way out. I told him that you were just worried about something going wrong on your wedding day. But anyway as I was talking to him about you, it hit me where I knew him from." Alivia kept talking. I asked her to just get to the point and she said that she would, so I sat back down to let her finish. "After I notified Eric that I knew him, he started threatening me so that I wouldn't tell you. I told him that if he looked close enough in my eyes he would see no fear and he did because then what he said next I didn't expect. Alivia said as she looked up at me. I looked back at her begging her to tell me no matter what it was. "He said that if his sister would have had that abortion like he told her to, then you wouldn't be here and his life would be perfect." Alivia blurted out with a tear running down her face. "Wait, what, so you knew? Wait, I'm confused Alivia." I told her as Stan tried to walk over and comfort me as well, but Zavier wouldn't let him. "Kait, I knew him from when I use to live with my foster mother name, Kym, and he use to come over to have sex with her. He knew that I remembered and after I told him that I was going to tell you then maybe tell his wife, I guess he got frustrated and just spoke without thinking." She kneel in front of me. "It's not making sense. Why would he say that?" I asked her with tears rolling down my face. "Baby, he does have sort of a drinking problem and there's an old saying that a drunk man tells no tales." I couldn't help but agree with my future husband, but I didn't want too. Everything was just a mess, my life was a mess. Just when I thought my life was almost perfect, it turned out that I was living a lie.

CHAPTER 15

I wasn't sure why I wanted to be around Keith whenever I got emotionally stressed. I guess because he just understood me in a way that Stan and Zavier couldn't. I wasn't surprised when he didn't refuse my offer of me coming by. It had been months since we've seen or spoken to each other, but at that time we both agreed that it would be for the best. I tried to clean my face up before I got out of the car. I didn't want to have any boogers or makeup all over my face in case he tried to kiss me. I knocked on the door a few good times trying not to be so eager, but when Keith opened the door it was as if I was pushed into his arms. He immediately held me tight and closed the door and waited for me to let go. I don't know how long I held on to him, but I can tell it was longer than a minute. "You don't have to talk about it if you don't want to." He said as he walked me over to his love seat. I knew he did this so we would be sitting close to each other and honestly I didn't mind it at all. "Keith, I just found out that Eric..." I started to say before I got choked up. "Hey, calm down. Take a deep breath and relax. Do you want some water?" He offered. I told him that I really needed some tequila, but he refused to serve it to me and gave me water instead. "Eric is my uncle." I blurted out after I took a few sips of water. Keith was silent and looked at me with confusion. "What do you mean your uncle? How is that possible?" He asked. I then started from the beginning from where I told Stan that Eric had molested me as a child all the way up into how I ended up at his house. "Come here, shh...it's gonna be okay." He said as he opened his arms for me to lean in. "No it's not Keith. My whole life is a lie, my childhood was stolen from me. As far as I know everyone has been keeping a secret from me and I can't trust anybody. I mean Alivia even knew and didn't even tell me." I told him as I was wiping my face with my hands. "Well, I'm pretty sure that she would have eventually told you. I don't think she wanted to be the person to give her best friend bad news when she saw that you were happy." Keith said as he was helped me wipe my face.

I started questioning Keith in my head and wondered if he was hiding anything because he just seemed too good to be true. "Can I trust you?" I asked Keith. "You must do if you're here alone with me." He responded. "Just answer the damn question." I yelled as I got in his face. "I'm not answering that because you already know the answer." He replied as he tried to get me to sit back down. "Don't touch me! You men think ya'll are superior to women and that we are supposed to bow down to you." I said as I pushed him against the wall. "What the hell are you talking about?" He asked me. "Ya'll are all the same. Nothing ass, no good men." I said as I pushed his head against the wall. "Listen, I know you upset right now and

I understand that, but you not gonna keep putting your hands on me like that." He said with a stern tone to his voice. "I'm not scared of you and you not gonna do nothing, but take it." I said as I had both my hands up to push his head again into the wall, but he had grab them both. "Let me go! Now!" I shouted. When he did release me I was even madder and went full speed at Keith. But, he ended up picking me up and pushing me against the wall and as he did this I noticed that my hands were pinned over my head and he was reaching in my pants. "What are you doing?" I asked him with a soft but yet still angry voice. "What you been wanting me to do since the first day we met." He said as he put his fingers inside of me. I tried to pretend that I wanted him to stop and that I didn't want it, but he ignored all of that. "Keith, stop...." I moaned as he kissed my lips below. It was feeling better than the first time he did it.

He then picked me up to take me upstairs to his bedroom. I told him to put me down and to stop it, but he just looked at me in my eyes and started kissing me to make me shut up. Ah, he knew exactly what he was doing and he was doing it very well. As he undressed me, I couldn't help but notice how wet I was and he hadn't even put it in yet. He noticed it too because he went back down and licked me again. By this time, my legs were on his shoulders and his hands were up under my ass. Every time he licked me in a certain spot, I twitched and he held me so tight to let me know that he wasn't letting me go nowhere. "Yes, that feels so good. Right there....right there...yes. I'm about to cum.....hmmmm....I'm about to cum…" I was moaning out as he was licking and sucking me. "Cum baby.....cum. Let it out. Don't hold it. Cum! Cum!" He kept repeating in between licks. He knew that I had climaxed as my legs were fully wrapped around his neck and I held his head in my hands. That's when he put it inside of me and I wasn't ready. Whoever said all white men had a small penis lied, I felt his man pretty good inside of me. "I'm sorry baby. Did that hurt?" He seemed to be apologetic "Just a little, but I can take it." I replied back. "I'll stroke you slow and promise to take my time." He whispered in my ear and leaned in to kiss me. I swear this was a black man trapped inside of a white man's body. Keith didn't want me to do anything when we had sex. He wanted to satisfy and please me with every touch, stroke and lick. "You feel so good baby." He said as he placed my legs on his shoulders. I then told him to bend me over and he didn't have a problem with flipping my little ass over. He had me gripping the sheets as he was hitting it from the back. "You gonna take it. Where you going? Don't run." He said as it was beginning to be too much and I tried running away, but he had his hands on my hips and was holding on for dear life. "Keith, I can't take it. Take it out, take it out." I kept repeating to him. But, he ignored me and told me that I was gonna take it and I did until we both ended up cumming at the same time. I knew what we did was wrong, but it felt so good. I guess I had understood why people say doing the wrong things may feel good, but it doesn't make it right.

I wasn't sure how many times I came after the fourth round of sex. He could really go all night, but I knew I had to go home to Zavier. "So, where does this leaves us?" Keith asked "Um, friends still I guess." I said as I picked up my clothes. "Kait, stop lying to yourself. Honestly, you don't feel anything between us?" He asked me as he got out the bed to catch me before I started putting my clothes on. "I'm engaged to Zavier and we're supposed to get married in a few months. You're a great guy and I enjoy our time together, but..." I said before Keith interrupted and asked if it had to deal with him being white. "Seriously? No, it has to deal with the fact that I am with someone and I love him." I told him as I jerked away from his grip to put on my clothes. "Obviously, you don't love him that much since we just made love." He taunted as he walked away to get his clothes. "Made love? We just had sex and that's it. Nothing more than just plain sex. And who seduced who here? It sure in hell wasn't me." I said to him rudely. "Oh, don't act like you didn't want me to and that you didn't enjoy that. You've wanted me from the first moment we saw each other." Keith blocked the doorway. I told him that he was so full of himself and I regretted sleeping with him. "Oh boy. If Stan ever found out about this I would not hear the end of it." I said to myself with a chuckle. "Well, I think you should tell him." He said to me as I pushed past him to get downstairs. "Are you kidding me? I'm not telling Stan jack. He would not let me live this down because I always be on him on how he sleep with anything with a pulse. No offense." I said to Keith as I searched for my shoes. "I wasn't talking about Stan. I was talking about Zavier." He handed me my shoes. I asked him if he was high or if he just completely lost his mind. "If you guys really love each other, then no matter what the other does ya'll can make it work. Plus, you don't wanna start a marriage off with a lie." I didn't respond to Keith as his words pissed me off even more. I loved Zavier and wanted to marry him more than anything in the world. But, then I started thinking if it was possible for me to love Zavier and have feelings for Keith all at the same time. "Look, just forget this ever happened." I told Keith as I headed to my car. He didn't respond, but the look in his eyes assured me that he wasn't going to say anything because I knew that he didn't want to hurt me.

I didn't sleep at all last night and it was really showing. My body was so restless and my mind was so confused. There was a million and one questions and thoughts running through my head about the events that took place the day before. "Baby, you okay?" Zavier asked me as he rolled over to kiss me. "Yeah, I'm fine." I forced the words out of my mouth. "No, you not. I can see it in your eyes that you are not fine. Listen, baby, I am here and I'm not going anywhere." He said as he kissed me. I then felt his hands going into my panties and that's when my eyes started to tear up. To think that I've cheated on him and he has been nothing, but good to me. "Aww baby it's okay to cry. You're hurting inside and it hurts me to see you like this." He sat up to pull me on his chest. "I just wanna die. No matter how hard I try, I can't get this out of my head. It just hurts so much baby. It

feels like a knife is in back and someone keeps taking it out and putting it back in over and over again.
I'm bleeding to death and I don't wanna feel this...."
I said as I was cried like a baby with tears continu-
ously running down my face. Zavier told me not to
ever say something like that again and that he needed me and didn't know what he would do if he lost me
again. I could hear his voice cracking as if he was trying to hold back from crying when he told he wished
he could do something to take the pain away. "Just
being here with me is enough baby. I love you." I told
him as I kissed him. "I love you, too, and don't ever
leave me again like you did last night. I was scared
that you might have...never mind. Just answer your
phone or text me the next time you leave like that.
I was worried about you." He kissed me some more
and tried to make love to me again. But, I pushed him
away and told him that I wasn't in the mood. "Baby,
I need to tell you something." I told him. "The answer is yes. Whatever you want or need the answer is
yes." He said as he continued to kiss me to get me to
change my mind about making love. "Zavier, please.
I'm serious. I need to tell you something." I repeated
again as I pushed him away once more. "I'm listening
baby." He said and kissed my hand. He was making it
so hard for me to tell him what I did. "Don't be mad.
Promise you won't get upset with me." I stated to him.
"Baby, I can never get upset with you." He said. "Well,
last night while I was out. I was really upset and..."
I hesitated with a pause. Zavier was quiet as he was
waiting for me to finish. "What I want to say is that...I
don't want to have kids. I know you do, but I can't. My

life is so screwed up and I don't wanna raise a child in my messed up life." I informed Zavier. I know that it wasn't the truth, but as I was looking at him it just didn't feel like it was the right time. "Baby, it's okay. I just want you to be happy." He stated as he kissed my forehead. "How about breakfast in bed?" Zavier offered. I nodded my head up and down and waited for him to leave before I started crying again. He didn't deserve this and I was a bitch for doing this to him. I just hoped that when I did tell him that he would forgive me and we could move on with our lives.

After I recuperated for a week, I decided to get back to work. I wasn't worried about any work not getting done because the person I left in charge of my work, was a male version of me who was all about work and that was only because he wanted to be the interim boss whenever I was off. I knew that there was a risk of me having a break down at work and that's why I made sure I did everything in my power to be confined to my office for the rest of the day. "Hello?" I said as I answered my phone. "Hey, babe it's me. I just wanted to check on you." Zavier said. "I'm doing good so far. What number are you calling me from?" I asked. "I'm at work. It's my hospital emergency phone." He said. "Well, I'm walking in the building now, babe. Thanks, for checking up on me." I said as I was bounced up the steps. "Of course my love. Have a good day, and I love you." He said as I heard his name paged over the intercom emergency surgery. I was so blessed to have a man like Zavier. I knew that there wasn't anything that man wouldn't do for me.

As the elevator doors opened, I notice that no one was at their desk. I figured they were in a meeting as I heard voices coming from the board room. I decided to place my things down and go join the meeting just to see what I've missed or what I needed to fix, but when I got there I saw a banner outside the door which read, "congratulations" "What the hell is this?" I said as I opened the door to discover a baby shower going on. "It's a baby shower." Carmen responded. "Timothy, I put you in charge because I just knew that you were going to keep it together, but I was wrong. You can go home." My tone of voice let him know that was fired. "That is unnecessary. It's not that serious. It's just a shower and we're almost finished. We decided that this would be considered out lunch break and when it was time for lunch that we would all work through it. " Carmen said as she struggled to get up with her belly poking out. I then told Carmen she was fired as well as one girl started to open her mouth, but I quickly informed them that if anybody else disagreed with my decision that they could leave, too. "I want this room cleaned up now and everyone back to work in fifteen minutes. I see now that I can't be off anymore because once you let a caged dog out they act like they don't know how to behave.

After I had got caught up on some of my work, I decided that I was going to call Alivia to see if she had made it home safe. She had been with me this entire week. Stan did try, but I know that the chemistry between him and Zavier isn't good so he's been keeping his distance. "Hey, are you home safe?" I asked

Alivia as soon as she said hello. "Yes I'm here. But, how are you? You don't sound like yourself." I could hear the concern in her voice. I told her what happened at work and she fussed and told me that it was too soon for me to be back at work. "I needed something to keep me busy. Otherwise, I would just be thinking about the same thing and that was just gonna make me feel worse" I told her. Although, she couldn't relate to my situation she definitely understood why I had to keep my mind busy at all times. "There's something else going on I can feel it. Isn't there?" Alivia wouldn't let it go because all of a sudden I had become silent. I tried to assure her that nothing else was bothering me, but I couldn't hide it. "Kaitlyn, please don't do this again. I know you feel like you can't trust anybody, but you can trust me. So please don't shut me out." She said to me as she tried to hide the fact that she was getting teary eyed. I got up to shut my blinds in order to tell Alivia what I have done wrong. "Well, do you remember Keith?" I asked her. "Of course I do. That's why we fell out the first time." She responded back. "The night that we were all at Stan's house and I left. I was with him." I started off saying in order to figure out how to tell my best friend that I cheated. "Go on." She persisted. "I was hurt and mad and angry and upset and I just didn't know what to do or how to feel. I was vulnerable so don't judge me." I stopped to see if she was going to finish my sentence because I really didn't want to say what happened, but she didn't. "Things kind of got out of hand and we had sex." I told her with a low voice. "Okay." She said politely. "Okay? That's it? No fussing or saying how wrong it was?" I yelled at her. "Kait, you are a grown woman who can do whatever you want. You know whether it was wrong or not and I'm not here to judge. But, how do you feel about Keith?" I told her it was a mistake and that I loved Zavier and wanted to marry him. She didn't fuss with me this time about it instead she only said she was happy as long as I was happy with whatever decision that I made. It felt good to know that she was supportive of me and that she wasn't judgmental.

"I thought I told you not to call me unless I called you." Zavier said to Carmen as he answered his phone. "I know, but this is important." "What the hell is it? I'm busy right now." He was very standoffish. "Listen, I just thought you wanna know that you're soon to be wife isn't as perfect as you think she is." Carmen said to Zavier. Carmen saw Kaitlyn on the phone and knew something was up when she closed her blinds. So she decided to put her phone on mute and conjoin it to Kaitlyn's phone and that's when she heard it all. "What are you talking about? I don't have time for your games today." Zavier shouted out. "Look bastard first your fiancée fires me and then has the nerve to cheat on you. So, how does it feels to be on the other side?" Carmen asked as she laughed a little. Zavier was silent because he didn't believe what she was saying. "Does the name Keith sounds familiar?" Carmen said as she enjoyed the thought of ruining his plans because she wanted him to herself. "Go straight home and I'll come see you when I get off." He instructed her. She told him that she loved him, but he didn't hear because he hung up and dialed Kaitlyn's phone to see if what Carmen said were true.

CHAPTER 16

I decided that I had worked enough for the day and called Stan to see if I could come over and see him before he went back to his real home. "Of course, you can cum over and you know that you are more than welcome to visit me in Cali." He said as he talked dirty in order to get me to laugh. I would have to admit that they did always work and it might just be because they were so corny. "Well, let me finish sending out these emails and I'll be on the way." I told him. "Mexican?" He asked as in reference to food. "You mean the "BG's?"" I said back as in reference to bubble guts whenever I ate Mexican food. "And? I got more than one bathroom and plenty of tissue and air freshener?" He said with a laugh. I told him that it was fine as I hung up. Even after all that has happened in a week I could say that today was starting to feel like a good day.

I heard a knock at my door, but ignored it because it was locked and I was trying to get out of the office within the next fifteen minutes. Then the knocks became louder and louder and I jumped to curse whoever it was being an ass. "If I didn't answer and the door is locked that means..." I paused as I saw Zavier standing at the door. "Why did you lock your door?" He asked as he walked in my office. "Well, I was trying to get out of here because I gotta be somewhere in a few minutes." I replied and sat back down at my computer. "Where you going?" He asked me as he sat in a chair in front of my desk. "Uh, nowhere special just lunch." I told him as I was trying to concentrate on making sure I sent the right emails to the right person. "Mind if I join?" He asked with his hands folded. I told him that I was invited and not him. I guess he didn't take it as a joke because he pushed the chair back from him and demanded that I tell him who I was going to lunch with. "Have you lost your mind?" I answered as I sat back in my chair. "No, but you gonna lose yours if you don't tell me who you going to lunch with." He said as he paced back and forth. I told him that I think that he should leave and I would talk to him later after he has calmed down. "Baby, I'm sorry. It's just that you've been attacked and this thing with Eric. I feel like it's happening to me and I don't know what to do with all this anger that I have." He told me as he tried to hold me and kiss me, but I wouldn't let him. "Like I said, we'll talk later on tonight when I get home." I scooted back to my computer to finish up my work. I heard him say that he loved me, but I was too disappointed in him at the moment to say it back. "I'll just see you when you get home." Zavier said to me as he left my office.

Zavier was furious as hell on the inside and was far from letting this go. He decided to go see Carmen in order to kill time, but he knew he had to find out if Kaitlyn really cheated on him or not. "Hey, it's me.

You are a sick bastard you know that." Zavier said to Eric as he heard him pick up the phone. "You gonna believe that mess? She use to always make up stories when she was kid. Why do you think that she hates me?" Eric quizzed Zavier. "Maybe because you're a child molester." Zavier shouted. "No, you bastard. She hates me because I was the only one who saw through all of her web of lies. How do you think she ended up in the crazy house?" Eric mentioned her mental instability. "Who cares? I got a problem." Zavier told Eric as he left out of the parking lot of the courthouse. Eric told him that he was getting tired of fixing his problems. "So, she slept with another guy? That seems like a personal problem to me. Plus, don't you got some thot knocked up?" Eric reminded Zavier of his own infidelity. "Don't worry about that I got that okay. It's our problem because I met this guy before and I saw how she looked at him and how he looked at her. She might change her mind about us." He told Eric. "What the hell is your problem boy? You don't know how to lay the wood down? You youngsters these days. Rule number one of the game, always keep your main bitch pleased so her mind doesn't wonder and stays at ease." He tried to educate Zavier. "Look, you better fix this or I'll tell her about the living will and what's in it. She'll believe me because I've just been caring so much about her and how I feel her pain and how angry I am." Zavier mocked Eric in a baby voice because he really didn't care what was going on with Kaitlyn. "Well, look who decided to grow some balls." Eric replied. "Just fix it." He told Eric as he hung the phone. Zavier knew Keith was going to become a problem and that he had to keep him away from Kaitlyn as much as possible.

I called Stan to make sure that I was at the right restaurant considering the fact that there were two, I didn't know which one he was. "Yeah, I see you." Stan said as I was trying to find somewhere to park. My phone buzzed again I knew it was Stan rushed me because he was ready to eat. "I'm coming, I'm coming." I said. "You are and you didn't invite me?" Keith replied. Something told me I should have looked down to see who it was, but I just knew it was Stan so I didn't bother looking. "My bad I thought that you were someone else." I told him. "Can you come over?" He asked. I couldn't believe my ears as to what he just asked me. True enough the sex was good, but we agreed to be friends and nothing more. "Who the hell do you think I am? I'm not a booty call or just some ass you think you can get whenever you want. Okay!" I shouted out to him. "Listen, I didn't ask for ass. I only asked if you could come over because I enjoy your company. I know you're getting married and I apologize for what happened between us. I know that we are friends, but does that mean that we can't see each other?" He responded. "Look, I gotta go. Let me think about it." I told him as I hung up the phone. I did want to see him, but I knew that every time we would be around each other that we would have sex because there was a sexual attraction between us and I couldn't allow that to happen.

I tried not to make it obvious that something was wrong when I was having lunch with Stan, but he knew me all too well. "Why are you so quiet?" He asked me. "Nothing the food is good. Haven't you heard the saying when someone is quiet while their eating it means the food is good?" He ignored my analogy and asked me again what was wrong. "I don't want you to judge me." I finally said with hesitation. "C'mon you should know me by now. I never judge or criticize anything that you do." He said as he reached over to hold my hand. As I started to tell Stan about my infidelity I felt a hand touch my shoulder. "Hey baby." Zavier said as he kissed my forehead. Stan went silent and excused himself as Zavier sat down. "What are you doing here?" I asked him in hopes that he didn't hear what I started to tell Stan. "Well, I was coming down here to pick up a few things to have a romantic dinner waiting for you when you got home and then I saw your car." He told me. "How did you know that was my car?" I asked him. "Your tag "BOSSY" gave it away." He laughed. I had totally forgot about my personalized tag that made my car stand out. "Listen, I didn't want to leave things like that. I guess I'm just jealous because you're so beautiful and I know that I have been unfaithful in the past so it just scares. It scared me that I may lose you because you may not see me for the man that I am today and remember the man from the past." He gazed into my eyes. "Baby, we're fine and we'll talk when I get home. Okay?" I told him when Stan came back to the table. We kissed and agreed that the conversation would continue at home later.

Stan was silent and didn't even asked me to finish what I was saying before Zavier showed up. "Don't you think that it was weird that he showed up like

that?" Stan asked me. "First, considering that this
is a small town, no. Second, don't you wanna know
why I am acting strange?" I asked. "I already know."
Stan insisted. "You do?" I asked him. He said that I
was acting strange because Zavier was hitting me.
"Whoa! You are way off." I told him with a laugh. "I
am? Then what's that on your arm?" He asked me. I
looked down on my arm and saw a bruise from when
Zavier was holding me earlier. "It was an accident. We
were arguing and things just got out of hand." I told
him without thinking how it sounded. "An accident?
That's what they all say." He said sarcastically. "Stan,
you wouldn't understand. Besides, when was the last
time that you actually had a meaningful relationship?
A meaningful relationship to you is any woman who
is willing to give you a piece of ass." I told him. "Wow!
When my real friend shows up tell her to give me a
call." He said as he placed the money on the table to
pay for lunch. I called his name as he walked away,
but he didn't even pretend to hear me. I was disappointed in myself about the things that I said to Stan.
It wasn't to hurt him or make him feel bad. I just was
upset at myself for how I acted the other night with
Keith.

I arrived home to see flowers on the doorstep. I
knew that Zavier would want to make love to me, but
I would have to soak in the bath tub before I give
him some just to make sure that I was back tight.
"Welcome home baby." Zavier said as he handed me
a glass of wine. "Thank you." I walked in to see rose
petals overflowing in the house. It looked like something from a movie and I was loving every minute of

it. "My name is Philip and I will be your servant." He announced in the worse British accent. I had to admit that it made me laugh and almost made me forget about my conversation with Stan earlier. "Well, Philip I would like a hot bubble bath and another glass of wine." I ordered and headed upstairs. "Your bubble bath is already waiting for your arrival and I will be up with that glass of wine momentarily." He headed to the kitchen. I could smell the aroma of lavender as I entered the master bedroom. As I entered the bathroom to touch the water, it was still hot just the way I liked it. I started undressing and heard Zavier coming in. "Madam, please allow me." He said as he sat the glass of wine down to help me get undressed. His British accent was terrible, but I was enjoying the role play. I got in the tub and Zavier handed me the fresh cup of wine. "How is the water?" He asked me. "Okay, you can stop now, babe. It was cute at first, but now it's annoying because you sound Jamaican and British." We both laughed as he agreed how his accent sounded. "What's wrong? Is the water getting cold?" He asked me. "No. I just feel like my whole life is falling apart and I'm not in control of it anymore." I told him as my eyes started to flood with tears. "I know baby and everything will be fine." He said as he started to get undressed. "What are you doing?" I asked him. "I'm going to make everything go away." He responded. I watched Zavier take off his pants and saw his manhood at full attention. It was getting me wet to know that I turned him on like that. He got in the tub and pull me on top of him with my glass of wine still in my hand, but took it and poured it on my chest. He licked the wine as it flowed down my chest and breast which was feeling good. He sat the glass on the counter top of the tub and started fingering me. I moaned and pulled his face close to mine so that we would kiss. "I wanna make you happy." He said while his finger went in and out of me. "I wanna make you whole. I wanna take away your hurt. I wanna take away your pain." He was whispering in my ear as I came on his finger. "I want him. I want him now." I told Zavier as I tried grabbing his man to put it in. Instead he picked me up and sat me right on it. I let out a sigh as I felt it going in and held on to him tight as he was moving up and down. My eyes was rolling in the back of my head as it was felt so good to me. "Baby, you feel so good." I was said over and over to him. "You do, too." He responded. I opened my eyes and saw it was Keith and immediately kissed him passionately. "You want this don't you?" He asked "Yes, give it to me." I told him as he placed me on the counter of the tub and placed my legs on his shoulders. "Tell me how bad you want it." He instructed. His tongue was wet and slippery and had me wanting more. I could hear him telling me how good I taste and how he wanted more of my cum. "Baby, please stop. I can't take anymore." I told him as he held on to my waist. "Give it to me. Cum in this mouth. I want more." He told me as he held on to my waist. I felt myself getting real tight, but decided to relax. "Ah, yes baby. Yes, give it all to me." He said. As I looked down I saw that it was Zavier all along and not Keith who was satisfying me. Also, the fact that Zavier made me squirt and not Keith. "Baby, why are you stopping?" I asked him as he sat me back in the tub and he was getting a towel for himself. "Are you satisfied?" He asked. "Yes, but what about you? You didn't nut." I stated. "It doesn't matter what I won't. I only want to make sure that you are happy and fully satisfied." "I'll let you finish your bath." He said as he kissed me before leaving. I did my best and held back my tears until he left because it was hurting me on the inside to know that I was unfaithful to Zavier. He didn't deserve this.

CHAPTER 17

I didn't feel like being at work today, but I had a diffi-cult case in a few weeks that I needed to prepare for. "Come in." I said as I heard a knock at the door. "Ms. Thomas, I hate to bother you, but may I talk to you for a minute?" Carmen said as she walked in. I didn't know why she was there and could care less. "You have ten minutes." I replied and pointed to a chair for her to sit down in. "First, let me apologize about having my baby shower here. It just that I don't have much family and I've gotten close to people here and kind of consider them to be my family. You of all peo-ple should know what that feels like." "Excuse me?" I was irritated with her. What I meant was, I heard you say Mr. Thomas wasn't your real father so I asked someone who has been here awhile and they told me that you were adopted by them." Carmen stammered as she tried to cover up the fact that it was Zavier in whom she got her information "Oh, yeah. I guess some of the old heads who were here when Eric was still working would know that information." I said as I asked her if she wanted anything else. "Well, I was hoping that I could have my job back I really need it to support me and my baby." She informed me. "Isn't that what your baby daddy for?" I asked. "I have a boyfriend and not a baby daddy as it's complicated." She told me. "Oh, so you mean he got another woman or are you the other woman? Anyway it doesn't matter because you're not getting your job back. You will get your pay all the way up until your contract ends so that should help keep you on your feet for a while until you can find a job." My tone was distracted as I hoped she would take that as a sign and leave.

Carmen wanted to tell Kaitlyn that she was the other woman and not her, but she couldn't because she knew that she would lose everything. "Thank you for your time." She thanked Kaitlyn after closing the door behind her. "Hello?" Carmen said as she answered her cell phone. "Hey, babe I'm at your house. Where you at?" Zavier asked her. "Funny you should ask because right now I'm standing outside the door of your future or soon to be future ex-wife office." She told him. "What in the hell do you think you are doing? How many times do I have to tell you this?" Zavier raised his voice. "Who are you yelling at? Because I will go right back in the building and tell her everything." Carmen said as she walked down the stairs of the courthouse. "I thought you were in her office? It doesn't matter okay, I'm sorry. I came to your house to treat you to lunch and you weren't here and it's just been a busy day at work that's all." He stated. "Well, I was in her office trying to get my job back, but that didn't work. I'll be there in about thirty minutes I gotta stop by the pharmacy. Love you." Carmen told Zavier. Zavier knew that he had to make this marriage to Kaitlyn happen soon, but didn't know how without making it look suspicious. I was so glad that the day was almost over with. I was really looking forward to getting home to Zavier and having a nice hot relaxing bath, but that fantasy quickly disappeared when I heard a knock at my door. "It's open." I said as I was preparing myself to come home. "Glad I was able to catch you before you left." Cassandra said. I wasn't at all happy to see her, in fact I didn't care to see her or Eric ever again. "What are you doing here?" I asked her. "Well, you haven't answered any of my phone calls." She said. "We have nothing to talk about." I said to her with a firm tone in my voice. "Kaitlyn sweetheart you gotta believe that if I knew what was going on I would have done something. It hurts me to even think that you believe that I would willingly let something like that continue to happen." She expressed with tears in her eyes. "Cassandra, I am trying to move on with my life and I don't want anything to do with you or that bastard, Eric. I am planning a wedding and that is stressful enough without adding you and him to the picture." She frowned at the fact that I was getting married so I asked her what her problem was with Zavier. "Kaitlyn, you are a very smart girl and I can't say too much without fearing for your life and safety, but have you asked yourself why you're still here working at the firm after all that has happened? Don't you think that knowing what kind of man Eric is that he would try to make your life miserable?" She questioned. I would have to admit that I did think about that, but I knew he didn't have anyone else to run this company like I did and since I've been winning my cases it shows that I am worthy of owning the firm. "It really doesn't matter because once Zavier and I are married, I'm moving and going to start my own law firm so I can put people like Eric behind bars." I promised her as I headed to the door to let her know that I was leaving and she should too. "I see. Well, honey just be careful. You are so sweet and honest and sometimes that is your downfall. It makes it hard for you to see what is really going on around you. Watch your surroundings especially at home. I've been married to the same man since I was seventeen and thought I knew him, but that just shows you never truly know someone until you're watching them from a far." Cassandra said with a tear rolling down her face. I had no idea what the hell she was talking about. Personally I thought she was high on something because what she said to me didn't make any sense. It didn't matter anyway because no one was going to change my mind about anything that I did. I decided that I was going to take control back over my life and Kaitlyn was going to do whatever Kaitlyn felt like doing.

"Hey babe, what time are you leaving the office today?" Zavier asked me. "Well, I'm actually walking out to my car right now. Baby, I'm so stressed." I complained to him. "Don't be stressed baby; it's not good for you." He me replied with concern. "I know but I just want this wedding to be perfect." I told him with a sigh. "Well, let me ask you this. What if we didn't have a wedding? Would you be upset or disappointed?" He probed. I had to really think about how I felt about not having a wedding because it has always been my dream to have a day all about me. "Well, baby you know that I've always wanted a wedding, but I can understand your concern about it stressing me out. How about if we cut down on how many people we invited." I suggested "It's whatever you want my love. I just can't wait until I make you Mrs. Zavier Price." He blew a kiss over the phone. I voiced my excitement as well and that I would be there shortly.

As I searched for my keys in my purse, I heard someone call my name. When I looked up it was Keith. "God enough already!" I yelled out as I thought God was punishing me because first it was Carmen, then Cassandra came by, and now Keith. "Can I talk to you for a minute please?" He asked. I ignored him and continued to look for my keys. "Kaitlyn don't do this. Can we please talk?" He asked again and I still continued to ignore him. "Dammit Kait!" He yelled as he grabbed and kissed me. I tried pushing him away, but my lips wouldn't let go. "Bastard! Don't you ever touch me again." I screamed as I yanked away from him. "You didn't resist." He said with a smirk. "Go to hell." I demanded and wiped my lips. "Kaitlyn, I love you. I don't know when it happened, but I've never felt this way before about anyone else, and I know you feel something too." He told me as he rubbed his face where I hit him. "You was just a cut buddy okay. I shouldn't have done it and I regret it. It was just sex, nothing more." I told him as I had finally found my keys. "Let me just say this and then I won't ever bother you again." He begged for me to stay to listen. "What?" I replied as I rolled my eyes. "Why is it

that each time you've called me it was because you
needed to be comforted? Don't you think you should
be able to find that comfort with the one you love?
Why is it that you allowed me to make love to you
and then kiss you just now? Your mind is saying one
thing, but your heart is controlling your body." He
said. "Look, my heart belongs to Zavier not you." I
told him in belief that he didn't know what the hell he
was talking about. "Okay. Your heart may belong to
him, but your love belongs to me and you know this.
That's why you don't wanna see me anymore. I've noticed that every time I come around, you keep an arm
length distance, you try not to look me in my eyes,
and you're breathing changes. Why is that?" He requested to know. "Keith, you are a nice guy and you
deserve happiness, but just not with me. I'm sorry." I
told him as I got in the car before he could see me
cry. Why are you doing this to me, God? Why? I've
been through so much already and I just can't take
anymore. Please stop. I was somewhat angry at God
for how my life had turned out and all the bad things
that has happened to me. I just wanted my life to be
perfect and I was determined to get it there.

I couldn't wait to tell Alivia about the news between me and Zavier. We had decided to elope in Las
Vegas and I wanted my two best friends to be there. I
decided to cancel my wedding plans after all because
I didn't have any family anymore. I had completely
cut myself off from Cassandra and Eric. "What about
his family?" Alivia asked me as I asked her to be my
maid of honor. "Well, they were upset, but respected
our wishes. Just as long as when we got back that we

would allow them to throw us a reception." I told her. "That's nice of them to do and of course I'll be there, but have you told Stan?" She asked with a pause. "No, I haven't yet and I really want him to be there. I'm pretty sure he's over the fact that I am marrying Zavier by now." I told her. "I'm sure too. I mean, everyone deserves a second chance. But, let me ask you something and please don't get mad." "I'm listening." I stated. "Are you rushing into this because of Keith?" She. I don't know what made her ask me that silly question and why would she ask me that. "No, I love Zavier and I want to spend the rest of my life with him. I want to finally be happy and put all this behind me." I hope she could hear the firmness in my voice. She apologized and told me that she didn't mean to make me upset. I knew Alivia meant well, but sometimes she got under my skin.

I felt like it was ridiculous for me to fall in love with someone who I've only known for half of a year. Plus, I'd known Zavier a lifetime, and after all, we were supposed to get married before so it would only make sense for me to marry him. I quickly put Keith out of my mind as Zavier was entering the kitchen. "Have you called them yet?" He asked me. "Well, I called Alivia and of course she is going to be there. I haven't called Stan yet." I told Zavier. "Well, babe, all I can say is that a true friend would want you to be happy no matter what and if Stan can't do that then maybe he's not that good of a friend." He kissed my forehead before going to work. I agreed with Zavier to a certain extent, but wasn't going to give up on my friendship with Stan.

CHAPTER 18

Zavier was dressed to go to work, but he wasn't really going. He had unfinished business with Keith and knew he had to get it taken care of if he wanted his plan to succeed all the way through. He was prepared to take out his competition as he arrived at Keith's house. "Who is it?" Keith asked as he heard a soft knock at the door. Zavier didn't say a word and only knocked again. Keith thought it was Kaitlyn and decided to open the door without even peeping to see who it was. "What the hell do you want?" Keith asked Zavier. "I want you to keep your filthy ass away from my fiancée." Zavier. "Sure, but I don't think that she can keep away from me." Keith responded sarcastically as he tried to shut the door on Zavier. "You son of a bitch." Zavier said as he reached for Keith's neck to choke him. As they both fell to the floor, the door had closed shut. "Stay the hell away from her!" Zavier yelled again. Keith had punched Zavier in the face twice in order to get him off. "Get the hell outta here before I call the police." Keith said with a threat. "Like hell I will." Zavier replied as he charged him again in a rage. Keith had taken two blows to the stomach from Zavier before punching him with three blows of his own. "I don't want to fight you anymore. Now leave!" Keith instructed to Zavier. But Zavier refused to leave until he felt like Keith had enough so he ran full speed ahead at Keith and knocked them both onto the kitchen table. "What the hell is your problem, man?" Keith shouted as he flipped Zavier over and he landed on the floor. "Get your ass outta here right now before I call the police." Keith said again. "No! Now you listen to me you bastard." Zavier pointed his gun at Keith. "You're going to get out of town and never to come back or else next time I will pull the trigger." Zavier told Keith. Keith agreed, but told Zavier that if Kaitlyn really loved him then he shouldn't feel threaten. That had pissed off Zavier and he cocked the gun back to let Keith know that he wasn't playing. "Alright, alright I'll leave." Keith said to Zavier. Zavier had moved closer to Keith to ensure that he knew that he meant business, but Keith had reached for the gun as Zavier was distracted by the doorbell. As they struggled and scuffled with the gun throughout the kitchen it caused them to both hit the floor and the gun went off. "Oh my God! Keith! Keith! You're bleeding" Cassandra said as she rushed in after she heard the gun go off. "No, mom I'm fine. It's not my blood." He told her. "Zavier? Get up man." Keith said as he tried to shake him. "Look." Cassandra said as she pointed to the gunshot wound that Zavier took to the chest. "Alright we gotta call the police mom." Keith said. "No, son. We need to fix this." She told him. "It was an accident. He had a gun on me and it went off as we both struggled for it." Keith explain to her. But Cassandra started to tell Keith the entire story of why she wanted him to get Kaitlyn to fall for him and the plans that Eric and Zavier had schemed up. "Mom, I don't care about the money. You do!" He shouted at her. "You really do love her. Don't you son?" Cassandra asked him. Keith was silent as he thought about what to do next. "This is perfect. You really do love her, and how do you think she would feel if she found out that you killed the man that she loves? This is your chance to be happy and have what you want because deep down you know she loves you, too." Cassandra convinced Keith as she knew this would change his mind about calling the police. "Fine, we gotta make this look good." Keith told her. Cassandra told Keith not to worry and that she knew a guy who would fix this within a heartbeat. They both agreed to not speak of this to anyone nor to speak to each other in public because no one knew that Cassandra had a son and his name was Keith.

I had just got of court when I was told that I had an emergency phone call. My heart immediately went to racing as I thought about the worst thing that might have happened. "Hello?" I said. "Kaitlyn?" A woman's voice responded. "Yes, this is she. How can I help you?" I asked. "I know you're not going to believe this, but I'm your mother." The woman said to me. I stayed silent until I was able to get up and close my door to my office. "Um? Did you call me a few months ago?" I asked her. "Yes, I did and I don't have a lot of time, but listen." She paused as it sounded like she was waiting for someone to stop listening to her conversation. "Okay?" I replied back. "I'm your real birth mother. I don't have the time to explain, but your un-

cle Eric which is my brother, he put me here." She
stated. "Put you where?" I asked her even though I
didn't believe a word she said because I was told that
my birth mother died of a drug overdose, thus the
reason I never talk about her. There's nothing good
about having a drug addict for a mother. "In jail." She
whispered. "Okay, lady I don't know how much Eric
paid you to call me to get me to go crazy, but it's not
working." I told her as I was getting ready to hang up
until she called me by a nickname that only one person knew. "What did you say?" I asked her and hoped
she would say the wrong name. "Kait Bear." She repeated. "No one knows me by that name except for
my mother, but she died when I was four." I told her
as I was feeling confused. "No, honey. That's when
everything happened. You lost me and your grandfather around that time. Don't you remember?" She
asked me. I told her that I really can't say that I do because when I was in the mental institution, they said
that I had blocked all my childhood memories because I was traumatized by it. "Listen, I gotta go but,
if you have time can you come see me? I would love
to see you honey." She asked. I jotted down all the
information I needed after telling her I would think
about it.

When I hung up the phone, I didn't know what to
think or feel; however, I was feeling pain in my chest.
The question of whether she could have been my
mother or not kept replaying in my head, and just
the thought that Eric put her in jail made me even
madder. I know that hate is such a strong word, but
I hated Eric for how my life turned out. It was his

fault that I was in the crazy house and it was his fault that my life was so screwed up. He was to blame for all of the wrong that happened to me and the fact that he didn't feel like he did anything wrong, was the worst feeling. Before I realized it I had dialed Keith's phone. "What's wrong?" He asked. I tried to talk, but I was getting choked up from the crying. "I'm coming." He told me as he hung up the phone. I wanted to tell him no, but I needed to see him. Was Alivia right about me having feelings for Keith? I knew I could call Stan, but he lived in another state so he wouldn't have been able to comfort me physically. I needed to be held and I wanted Keith to be the one to hold me.

"Sorry, to bother you. But, there is a gentlemen here who said that it is urgent that he speaks with you." The receptionist announced over the intercom. "Send him in." I said with the little voice I had left. Keith didn't knock, but walked in and immediately went to holding me. "Talk to me what's wrong?" He asked. "My life is falling apart. I hate my life. Why should I be here anymore?" I asked as he helped me sit on the couch. "Don't talk like that. You have a lot to live for. You have a man who wants to spend the rest of his life with you and....." He wiped my eyes. "And I love you too. I know that you are getting married, and I don't want to ruin that. If it were the other way around, I wouldn't want another man perusing you." He kissed my hand. I don't know what made me do it, but I started kissing Keith as if we were in his bedroom. A small part of me would hope that Zavier would walk in and catch us which would cancel our engagement and that would take some of the stress away. I guess I just needed an excuse not to marry Zavier. I loved him don't get me wrong, but I had too much going on and I just needed to focus on myself. "Make love to me." I told Keith as I got up to lock the door and to get undress. He grabbed my hands and told me to stop as he kissed me. "You right. Not here. Let's go to your place." I ran and snatched my purse. "No!" Keith yelled as he remembered what happened earlier at his house. "Okay, well a hotel. I don't care. I just want you." I told him as I started kissing him passionately. He moaned heavily as my tongue massaged his. "Damn, I want you too baby. So bad! But, I can't." He pushed me back so I wouldn't feel his hardness. "Why?" I asked as I buttoned up my shirt. "It's not fair to you or me for us to keep doing this to each other." He said as he tried to push his man down because it was starting to bust through his zipper. "I'm confused here. You just said that you loved and wanted me and here I am throwing myself at you and you're pushing me away. Wow, I feel so embarrassed." I commented as I fixed myself together. "Don't be embarrassed. I want you, but I want you to myself and I know that's impossible because you're with somebody." He told me as he tried to rub my face. "I see. Well, I apologize for calling you and you're right we shouldn't do this anymore. I think that it would be best if you lost my number." I said as I was walking to the door. He begged me not to be like that, but he was being unfair. I understood what he was saying, but I didn't wanna hear it at that moment. "If that's what you really want then I can respect that, but just know that I will always be here. I'm gonna wait for you. No matter how long it takes because I know that we are meant to be and it will happen." He stated as he kissed me on my forehead. I don't see how I was going to get through this without having someone around me. I kept trying to reach Zavier, but I knew he was busy at the hospital. "Hey, um...you." I said looked at the new receptionist. "Tammy." She responded as she knew I didn't know her name. "Right. I'm gonna be gone for a few days. So, please only forward emergency calls to my cellphone." I told her as I got on the elevator. I felt myself on the verge of having a relapse of a nervous breakdown and even though me and Stan didn't leave on a good note I knew that he would want to know what was going on.

I decided to stop by the hospital to try to see if I could run into Zavier, just to let him know what was going on, but when I asked the floor nurse about him she said that he hadn't been in. "Are you sure that he hasn't been in today?" I asked her again. "Like I said. I'm looking at the work schedule and he wasn't on call today." She answered with an attitude. I started to cuss her out, but I was in a hospital and didn't need security escorting me out. "Okay. Well when is his next scheduled work day?" I asked her. She rolled her eyes and let out an annoying sigh as if it was really that hard to look up a schedule. "He's supposed to be in tomorrow." She stated as she folded her hands together. "Well, thank you. I hope that wasn't too difficult for your mind. By the way the proper English is, he is and not he's." I snapped back as I walked away from the desk. She had better be glad that I had things on my mind otherwise her feelings would have been hurt. "Hey, Zavier. I don't know where you are, but I've been trying to reach you. I thought that you were working today, but I might have just misunderstood you. Anyway, I'm flying out to California to spend some time with Alivia. I just need some girl time and you know that I don't have any here, so I'll just be gone for a couple of days. Call me as soon as you get this message. I love you. Bye." I politely left a message on his voicemail. I was really going to see Stan, but I knew that he would have been on the next flight out if I had said that. I hate lying and keeping secrets from Zavier, but every time I wanted to tell him the truth about me and Keith, he would do something wonderful and I just couldn't ruin the moment.

I decided to call Alivia to let her know that I was coming. "What's wrong, girl?" She asked. "Nothing, I just need to get away. Plus, Stand and I need to make up." I told her. "What was he mad about this time?" She wondered. I told her that I didn't even really remember which goes to show that it was probably something petty. "Well, I know I'll be gone all day tomorrow morning and afternoon. But, maybe we can do dinner?" She answered. I told her that I understood and didn't expect her to put her life on hold for me. "Girl, you are my bestie. Even though we don't live in the same state, I'm gonna be here for you regardless." She tried to make me feel better. I expressed how much I loved and appreciated her. "Same here. What did Zavier say about you coming out here?" She asked before ending the conversation. "Well, for one Zavier thinks that I am coming out there to see you, and for two, I haven't even told Stan that I was coming." I told her as I laid across the bed. "He's gonna be shocked to see you." She said with a laugh. "Alright, heffa I gotta get some sleep...I'll see you tomorrow." I rolled over to sleep on Zavier's side of the bed. "Bye, trick." She chuckled as we hung up the phone. I needed that little laugh with Alivia. It was moments like this that I wished that we lived close together, but I knew that she was only a phone call away and was always a listening ear.

CHAPTER 19

It may have been premature for me not to call to let Stan know that I was coming, but I didn't feel like explaining everything over the phone. I stood at the door waiting for him to answer as I heard his footsteps. "Hi?" A half-dressed woman said. I looked at her up and down like she could have at least put some pants on. "Who is it, babe?" I heard Stan shouted from upstairs. "I'm sorry. I should have called. I'll just come back." I said as I was turning around to leave. "Kait?" Stan said as he came to the door. "Surprise!" I yelled and held my hand out. "What are you doing here? Is something wrong?" He asked me. "Who is she?" The woman asked. "Can you go put your clothes on, please?" Stan pointed upstairs. As Stan was closing the door, I couldn't help but notice a tattoo on his shirtless body. "What is that?" I pointed out a he got closer. He looked down to see what I was talking about. "Not, that! That." I said as I tried to squeeze a laugh out instead of crying. "Oh, you gotta be more specific with me and you know this." He said with a chuckle as he told me it was an ex-girlfriend's name. "Why the hell? Never mind." I started to say, but just shook my head instead. Stan had noticed how quiet I got as I turned away from him to sit on the step. He sat down next to me and immediately placed his arm around my shoulder. I don't know how it happened, but I was weeping like a baby. You would have thought that I just got the worst news of my life. "Is she okay?" The woman probed. "I'm sorry, Stan. I should've called. I can call Alivia to come pick me up and just see you later. "No, I'm not about to let you leave like this. You need me and I told you that I was gonna be here for you no matter what." Stan proclaimed as he requested me to stay. I saw when he got up to tell the girl that he was with that this was important. "I understand. So, just call me later." She told him as she kissed him goodbye. "It was nice to meet you?" She stated as she was asking for my name. "I'm sorry. It's Kaitlyn." I said as I got up. "The Kait?" She said as she eyed Stan. "I'll call you later." Stan repeated again as he shoved her car. She smiled towards me as she got in the car. If you asked me, she seemed like she wasn't too bright almost dinky in a way. "What was that all about?" I asked Stan as he grabbed my bags. "Nothing." He said as he shook his head. I didn't ask again because there was enough going on and I didn't feel like playing the riddler today. "What are you looking for?" Stan asked as I opened all the cabinets. I didn't answer I just kept opening cabinets until I found what I needed. "Bingo!" I said as I had found his alcohol cabinet. I was looking for Tequila, but saw that he didn't have any so instead I just reached for the Crown and started drinking it down. "Kait. Enough." He tried to snatch the bottle away from me. "Move." I told him as

I pushed past him. "You've had enough. I can look at you and tell that you've been drinking already. Give it to me." He said as he held his hand out. I refused to give him the bottle because it was giving me the buzz that I needed.

I didn't wanna be awake and feel pain. "Dammit!" Stan said as he snatched the bottle away from me and some of it wasted on my shirt. "Look, what you did." I yelled at him as I held my shirt out. "You know what. I don't need this. There's a bar two blocks from here. I'm gonna get drunk off my ass and then maybe have sex with a stranger." I told him as I was taking my shirt off to find me a clean one. "No, you're not. Your ass is gonna sit right here and sober up and then we are gonna talk." He yelled back at me. I ignored him as I found me a shirt to put on. "Move outta my way." I told Stan as he was blocked the doorway. "Sit down. Sit down!" He yelled at me. "Who the hell do you think you are? You slept with plenty of women without caring. So, now I can't do it? Besides your little girlfriend didn't want me here anyway." I told him as I was still trying to move him out the way. I guess he had enough of me slapping him because he picked me up and threw me on the couch. "Get off of me! Get off of me! I hate you! Eric, I hate you!" I yelled as images of Eric face being on top of me started to flash before my eyes. With me tussling and fighting, it forced us to fall off the couch and ending up on the floor, but Stan still had his arms wrapped around me. He was trying to get me to calm down because I started hyperventilating.

I felt myself catching my breath as Stan was rocked me. He didn't ask me why I was acting like the way I was and I was glad because I was exhausted. "It hurts so much." I complained to him as I tried to relax. "I can't say that I know how you feel because I don't, but doing things like this isn't gonna make it any better. Getting drunk and doing things out of character will only make it worse." I felt his finger wipe my eye. "Can you make it go way?" I asked him as I sat up. "No, I can't make it go way, but I can be here with you. I can help you get through this. We don't realize how strong we are until we accomplish what people thought would tear us down." He said as he rubbed his hand through my hair. I stumbled a little as I tried getting up from the floor because it was starting to hurt my butt. "Easy." Stan guided me as he caught me before I could hit the floor again. "Your eyes." I said to him as I was looking at him face to face. "Yep, I have eyes and look you do, too." He said as he sat me down on the couch. "Their beautiful." I told him as I rubbed his bald head. "Okay? You're officially drunk." I heard him say as he laid me down on the couch. "I'm gonna get you some aspirin and water. Try not to fall off the couch." He told me. I knew at that moment this was my chance. I had the opportunity to see if anything was between me and Stan. "Sleep with me." I said to him as I stood fully naked in the den. "Here, take this and drink this." He said. "Make me feel better." I told him as I pushed him down on the couch to get on top of him. I started kissing him and rubbing his bald head in order to get him to give in. "Kait?" He said with a moan as I placed my hand in his pants. "Stop talking." I said as I started kissing him some more. "You don't know how long I've wanted this." He said as he wrapped his arms around me. "Don't keep me waiting then. Give it to me." I instructed as I pulled his manhood out which was saluting mighty well. I felt Stan hands caressing my ass as he started kissing me down my neck. For a second, a split second I had forgot what was going on in my life until Stan stopped. "Why are you stopping?" I asked him. "I can't. This is wrong. I can't do this." He said as he sat me on the side of him. "What? You scared your little girlfriend will find out? I won't tell her and I won't tell Zavier." I said as I got on my knees to pleasure him. I saw when his head went back on the couch as he felt my tongue on his man. "No!" He yelled out as he pushed me back. "What the hell? You sound just like Keith." I said with an attitude as I grabbed the blanket to cover myself. "Keith? Never mind I don't even wanna know. But, this is what I'm talking about. You're drunk. You don't wanna do this. It's just the alcohol." I heard Stan say as I ran to the bathroom to throw up. "I'm...tired......of ......people.....telling....me......what......" I kept trying to get out, but I kept throwing up. Stan placed a cold rag around my neck and pulled my hair back. I was feeling so horrible. My head was pounded and the only thing I could do was lay on the bathroom floor and hold the toilet.

I could taste vomit in my mouth as I got up from the cold bathroom floor. My head was pounding so bad that it prevented me from getting up. "Did we sleep well last night?" Stan asked me as he handed me a glass of water along with some aspirin. I couldn't say anything, but just moan. "I'll take that as a no. Well, anyway Alivia came by of course she was disappointed when she saw you like this." He stated. "What time is it?" I asked him as I was finally able to get up. "Um, it's a little bit after two." I knew when I walked into the Fourier, it was two in the afternoon. In a way I was glad because that meant I was able to sleep most of the hangover off. "I'm gonna take a bath and get cleaned up. Do you mind calling Alivia back and see what time she can come by?" I asked as I went upstairs. "Sure. Do you want something to eat?" He asked me. Ugh, just the thought of food was making me want to throw up again. I didn't answer him because I was too busy trying to get to the bathroom. I don't know what came over me the night before, but I sure in hell won't mix brown and white again. I was shocked that I hadn't received any missed phone calls. I knew that I wouldn't get a call from Keith anymore, but at least I thought Zavier would call. "The voicemail box is full, please try your call again later." The automatic voice to Zavier's cell phone said. I couldn't understand why I wasn't able to reach him and why he hasn't attempted to call me. It bothered me for a second and then I started remembering the main reason why I came to California.

I hoped that drinking coffee straight black would help, but it just made me sick to my stomach. "That's what your ass get." Alivia reprimanded me as she walked in the kitchen to find me with my head down on the table. "Please, stop yelling." I told her as it was sounded like she was speaking through a bullhorn. I rubbed the side of my head, but that didn't seem to help ease the hangover either. "Want another one?" Stan asked as he shook the pill bottle. "How many can I take?" I asked him before reaching for the bottle. "You can take two more, but then you gotta wait at least four hours before taking anymore." He said as he gave me two more aspirins. "I did not cancel my appointments today to watch you experience a hangover. You better start talking heffa." Alivia said. I saw Stan giving her a rude look, but it was normal to me. "Oh, GOD!" I said as I sat up and held my hand over my mouth. "Don't you dare do it. Take yo ass to the bathroom." Stan said as he pointed to the doorway. "No, I'm not gonna throw up. Last night?" I said as I started to remember. "What? Last night what?" Alivia said as she looked at me and Stan. "Nothing." Stan said as he rubbed his bald head. "Ya'll got about five seconds to start talking or the bitch in me is gonna come out." Alivia said as she had switched from professional to ghetto. "Stan?" I said as I wanted to talk about it, but he kept brushing it off. Instead he kept bringing up the things that I was saying while I was intoxicated. "Well, a drunk man never tells no tales." Alivia said as she pointing her finger at me.

I started from the beginning of everything and trying not to leave nothing out. Even, though they may have heard some of it, I wanted to be sure that I didn't leave nothing out. Tears kept flowing and flowing as I talked about the pain that Eric had put me through. I wouldn't let them comfort me because that just made it worse. "So, who blew up your car?" Alivia asked after I took a breather. "I don't know.

Maybe Eric. Nothing surprises me anymore about him." I told her in between sobs. "If I got this correct. Eric is really your uncle? He molested you as a child? Zavier cheated on you when ya'll was supposed to get married? You tried killing yourself leading up to you getting institutionalized? You slept with Keith and you might love him? Damn, girl I don't see how you standing. I would've gotten drunk, too." Alivia sounded sympathetic as she shook her head. Stan must've kicked her because I heard her say, "ouch."

"No, it's okay. Maybe I needed to hear that." I told Stan as I was wiped my eyes. "So, have you talked to Zavier?" Alivia asked. "Nope, I can't reach him and who can blame him for keeping his distance? I've been so needy lately. Oh and I almost forgot, some woman claiming to be my mother called." I said to them. "Wait? What? Now I need a drink." Alivia got up from the kitchen table. Stan was silent the entire time and who could blame him. I was a broken woman with a broken heart, I wouldn't even be friends with me. I got too much baggage that can ruin any relationship and friendship. I was damaged goods.

CHAPTER 20

Alivia thought that it would be a good idea if I got out the house for a while. I really think she did it because it was starting to get awkward between me and Stan. I didn't know what he was feeling because he wasn't saying anything. However, I knew that he cared because when before we left he gave me a huge hug and kissed me on my forehead. "What do you think is wrong?" I asked Alivia as Stan sat on his doorstep. "Honestly, he's hurting." Alivia said as she was backed out of the driveway. "He's hurting? I'm the one going through all this pain." I said. "You still don't get it? That man right there loves you. I mean really loves you. Zavier loves the fact of ya'll being back together, he's loving the past you. Keith is just lust, but that man right there is really in love with you." She said as we drove off. I wanted to tell her how wrong she was. I loved Stan, but just not in the way he wanted me too. I had feelings for Keith and knew that there could be more if I would allow it, but I was limited because I was with Zavier. I don't think that she really knew what she was talking about because I have yet seen her with a man nor have she mentioned a man. "Don't think just because I don't have a man that I don't know what I'm talking about. I know all of this from past experiences and that's why I choose to be single because a lonely heart is easier to deal with then fixing a broken one." She answered as a tear rolled down her face. I had to pause, like did I just say that out loud, or is this bitch psychic? "Let's not talk about men while we're out. Agreed?" She agreed. We had planned to do a girls night out minus the club. Our evening was gonna be filled with massages, pampering, and relaxation. Although, she probably was gonna enjoy it more than me because the only other thing I liked doing when I was stressed I did with Zavier, but more recently I did it with Keith.

Even though I was a week away from marrying the love of my life I couldn't help, but wonder if I was making the right decision. I know that I've told every-one how happy I was and that I didn't want anyone else; there was still a feeling that I had that wasn't filled. This may just be butterflies or cold feet and that I am making a big deal out of nothing. These thoughts was making it hard for me to enjoy my mas-sage. "So after all of that you have yet neglected to tell Stan about getting married to Zavier next week?" Alivia mentioned as we finished up with our mas-sages. "Did you not see the look on his face? If I told him that it would have crushed him even more. Be-sides, I don't think that it's gonna happen." I told her as I sat up from the massage table. "What? Listen, I'm gonna tell you this and its only because I love you and care for you." She said as she was fixing her hair back down. All I could do was roll my eyes and just think, lawd, what now? "Maybe you shouldn't get married and I mean like right now. You got a lot going on and I think that it is really important that you focus on yourself for a while." She advised. I told her that I appreciated her concern, but that I was a grown woman and capable of making my own choices. "Can I ask a question?" Alivia asked as were walked back to the ladies' locker-room. "Sure, why not? Because no matter what I say you gonna ask me anyway." I told her. "Never mind." She said as she was getting dressed. "No. No. Don't do that! You know I hate it when you do that." I told her and leaned up against the locker. "No, it's just gonna upset you and I don't wanna do that." She said as she waved her hand. "Alivia Zoe Parker!" I yelled out. She knew I was serious whenever I called her out by her whole name even when we were younger. "Okay! Okay! Here's what I'm thinking. You haven't been able to reach Zavier, right? I think that he can't handle everything that has been going on and decided to dip. But, that's just my opinion." Alivia shrugged her shoulders. I didn't respond because what she said just didn't make sense. Zavier had been so wonderful and what I was doing to him was unfair. I couldn't explain why I haven't been able to reach him, but I knew that it wasn't for the reason that Alivia said. But, maybe she was a little right about holding off on marrying Zavier. I was pretty messed up. Therefore, I didn't feel the need to tell Stan about us eloping at least not right now.

I was surprised to still find Stan sitting on his doorstep when we returned. I could tell that he's been in the house though because his clothes were different and he was drinking something. I knew it was alcohol, but I wasn't sure what kind. I secretly wished that he didn't wanna talk because I was exhausted from all that talking earlier that day and the massage just made me more relaxed. "Hey." I said as I stopped at the first step. "Hi." He said back in a very low voice. I could tell that he had been crying by how red his eyes looked. Alivia waved at Stan instead of speaking because she didn't wanna bother him. He wasn't rude, he gave her a head nod back. "Tomorrow, I may be able to do brunch depending on how needy my client will be." Alivia told me as we hugged. "Okay, just give me a call." I told her as I walked in. I heard Stan say something so I peeped my head back out the door, but he was talking to Alivia. I think that he knew that I was still at the door because he motioned for her to walk out to curb. I couldn't hear what they was saying so I didn't waste my time by trying to even pretend to know what they were talking about. This was my cue to go to bed, besides I still had a small hangover from the night before.

"Did she talk about me at all?" Stan asked Alivia. "Not that I can remember." She told him. "Are you sure?" He asked her again. "Yes, Stan I am sure. She really didn't wanna talk much especially after I told her that she shouldn't elope with Zavier." Alivia said before she knew it. "Elope? What the hell are you talking about?" Stan asked. "Nothing. I didn't say nothing." Alivia turned to walk away, but Stan had her at the elbow. "When was this supposed to happen?" He asked her as he looked up at the door to see if Kaitlyn was outside. "Please, don't let her know that you know. She would kill me." Alivia begged and clasped her hands together in a prayer. Stan agreed not to say anything because he didn't want to risk any small chance he had with Kaitlyn. "But, next week we were all supposed to go to Vegas, even you. She wanted to tell you, but didn't know how you would react." She said. "I gotta stop that wedding." Stan said to Alivia. "It may not happen. She hasn't been able to reach him." Alivia said. "Yeah! Cause he too busy with his side bitch." Stan blurted out. "You don't know that. Just because she hasn't spoken to him doesn't mean....wait......do you know something?" Alivia asked as she saw the look in Stan's eyes. "I'm supposed to be the one marrying her and not that son of a bitch. He's no good for her. Why can't she see how good I am for her?" Stan whispered. "You didn't answer my question. What do you know about Zavier that you're not telling me?" Alivia questioned as she folded her arm. "Nothing, I just know how he is and I still believe that he is cheating." Stan said in order to correct his mistake. "You're lying." Alivia told him as she was walked to the door of Stan's house. "Where are you going?" He asked her. "Oh, nowhere. I'm just gonna see if Kaitlyn would like to join this conversation." She said as she was getting ready to open the door. "What the hell is wrong with you, crazy ass?" Stan asked as he pulled her away from the door. "Well, if you won't talk to me then maybe you'll talk to Kaitlyn." She said as they walked back to the curb. "Alright, what I'm saying is that the last time I visited Kait, I did see him with a woman." Stan replied. "Okay? Is that a crime?" Alivia asked Stan as she was walking to her car. "Yes, if you're kissing and groping that woman." Stan said. Alivia paused with her door open to think about what Stan just said. "Listen, I know that you love her and want to be with her, but don't force it. You can tell her that Zavier may or may not be cheating, but she'll resent you for telling her. Why? Because she believes that she has a good man and you would ruin that fantasy for her." Alivia got in her car. Stan was surprised that Kaitlyn hadn't come to the door, but when he went in he found her asleep on the couch. He didn't wanna disturb her sleep so he just covered her up. "I love you." Stan said as he kissed her forehead. "I love you too, Keith." He heard Kaitlyn mumble in her sleep. He was disappointed that it wasn't his name she said, but was glad that it wasn't Zavier's name either. Stan decided to take Alivia's advice and let nature takes it course because he didn't wanna ruin his friendship by trying to build a relationship that may never happen.

It seemed mighty strange that Zavier hadn't called me back yet, so I decided to give him a call again. "Yes, can you let me know if Dr. Price is in surgery?" I asked the nurse in the ER. I waited as I heard her page for Zavier. "No, ma'am. It looks like he hasn't been in." The nurse replied. "What do you mean he hasn't been in?" I asked. "You're mistaken; Dr. Price isn't scheduled to work today." She sounded very confident. I immediately hung up the phone and started dialing Zavier's number. I didn't want to jump to conclusion because he had been so good to me, and I doubt that he would do anything to hurt our future together. On the other hand, I couldn't help but to think that maybe Alivia's theory was right. That he fled before it got tough, but I probably would've done the same thing. I must've called his phone probably ten times and still no answer. I knew that there had to be a good explanation as to why. "Still haven't talked to him?" Stan asked as he saw me dialing my phone. "Huh? No, I don't know what's going on, but something is telling me that something is wrong." I told Stan as I continued to dial his number. "Maybe he went to a convention and just forgot to tell you." Stan said as he sat down on the couch. "Maybe, but this isn't like him. I think I'm gonna fly out today." I told Stan as I got up. I wanted to throw my phone across the room so bad, but then if he called me back I wouldn't know because my phone would be broke. "If you're ready to go back I can take you to the airport. I don't have practice for another five hours, so I'm free." Stan extended his arms. "Aw, Stan I'm sorry. You've missed practice." I told him as I sat back down. I forgot that it was getting close to football season again and he had to practice. "No, don't be. I told you that I was gonna be here no matter what and I meant it. Besides when you're gone, I'll be there all day and all night to make up these last two days." He commented as he got up to go into the kitchen. I apologized to him one more time and immediately texted Alivia to let her know that I was leaving. I was praying that Stan was right and that maybe Zavier was just really busy and forgot to tell me, but something still wasn't just sitting right with me

"So, are you gonna just sit there and continue to act like nothing is wrong?" Cassandra said to Eric as she walked into his study. "What do you want me to say? That little bitch has got the entire town looking at me crazy as if I am some kind of criminal." He jumped up from his chair. "You know what? A year after we were married you told me that you wanted to get custody of your niece, but the state may not let you because your sister was on drugs and how she lied on you and told them that you were the one who was her supplier. I remembered how you cried every night about her and it broke my heart. But, none of that was true was it? All of that was a big act so that you and Zavier can get your hands on that money that your dad left her. That's right! I found the Will. He left everything to her." Cassandra said as she poured a glass of scotch. Eric was silent as he stood next to Casandra pouring him a glass as well. "And once I can talk to her again. I'm going to tell her everything and she will hate you even more." Cassandra said with a laugh. "Yes, you are right. My dad did leave everything to her and of course with the marriage of her and Zavier the husband is entitled to seventy-five percent of that and because of me letting Zavier know I would have been given fifty percent of that, but you're forgetting one thing my dear." Eric said as he took a sip of his scotch. "What?" Cassandra said as she took a sip of hers. "Your grandmother is old and senile. I remember a year after our marriage, too. See I remember a little boy that you said was your nephew who for some odd reason looked nothing like his parents, but just like you. Now, the damnedest thing was that on our five year anniversary your mother thought I knew all about it and just started talking about it freely." Eric said with a laugh. Cassandra didn't find anything funny about this conversation. "So, you see you got your hand and I got my hand. We'll see who has the best poker face." Eric said as he headed towards the door. "Oh and tell Keith don't be a stranger. Besides he's my step son who might be my son in law. Either way my dear we both win, so I advise you to just let it be." He said as he left the room. "Oh, I never fold my dear." Cassandra said to herself as she was thinking on how Kaitlyn was gonna respond to Zavier's death. She knew it was gonna hurt her, but knew that Kaitlyn would run into the arms of Keith and probably blame Eric for it. The key was getting Kaitlyn to find out about it without drawing suspension to herself or Keith. "Bring it, bitch." Cassandra said as she raised her glass in the air. She was preparing to win this game and enjoy the riches that came with it.

CHAPTER 21

There was still no sign of Zavier when I got to his house everything looked the same. "Hello?" I said as I answered my phone. "You've landed?" Stan asked. "Yeah, I'm sorry. I got here maybe about two hours ago. I had to stop by the office real quick." I told him. "Oh okay. Well, have you talked to him?" Stan asked. "No and it don't look like he's been here for a couple of days. I'm starting to get worried." I told him. "Hey, listen don't get upset okay. Like I said, maybe he had a doctor's convention he forgot to tell you about and he's been really busy and just haven't had a chance to get to you." Stan told me. "I hope you're right." I told him as I leaned over the counter. "In the meantime I don't want you way out there by yourself. So, I want you to stay at my old house." He told me. I had already been thinking about that and told Stan I was gonna get me a room at a Hotel. "Why are you wasting money?" He said. "Because I don't feel comfortable over there anymore now that I'm with Zavier, okay." He agreed and made me promise to call him once I got in my room safely. I had no idea what the problem was with Zavier, but I knew one thing that once his ass got back he had a lot of explaining to do.

Don't ask me why I was sitting outside the courthouse trying to go into work because I really don't know myself. I had plenty of vacation time, but I got tired of just looking at the four walls of the hotel room. Even though I was getting work done, I needed a different scenery besides the hotel room and after still with no word from Zavier, it had finally set in that he was gone. I realized that Alivia was right and that he had left me. I lost a good man and deserved it, especially after I cheated on him. I was feeling so bad that I changed my mind and decided not to go in to work, so I quickly sent an email to my new assistant to inform her that I had a business conference to attend. I knew it was lie, but considering the fact that I emailed her first thing this morning to let her know that I was back from vacation, I had to come up with something to let her know why I wouldn't be in all of sudden.

I didn't know what do without him anymore, I loved him and needed him to see me through my hurt. I could feel my chest getting tight as tears started came down my cheek. I tried to hold it in until I got back to my hotel room, but I was too upset to drive. Then, I heard a tap at my window. After my car got blown up, Zavier got me a new car and had the windows tinted so no one could see inside, but I could see out. I saw that it was Keith. "What?" I yelled. "Are you okay?" Keith asked. "I'm fine." I responded and sniffled. "I don't think that you are considering the fact that you've been sitting in your car for the past twenty minutes." Keith said. "So, what are you stalking me now?" I asked as I only had the window half way cracked. "Can you please let the window all the way down or get out the car?" He asked. I didn't want Keith to see me like this because then he would know that something is wrong. I quickly went to wiping my face and dabbing my eyes as make-up had ran everywhere. When I finally rolled the window down he was leaning on the car ready to see if I was really okay. "See I'm fine." I told him as I sat my hand under my chin. Before I knew it Keith had stuck his hand in to unlock my door. "What the hell are you doing?" I asked him as he opened it and pulled me out of my car. "Get your hands off of me!" I said as I was trying to push him away. He ignored my request and proceeded to hold me. "Stop! Stop it! Get off of me! Leave me alone!" I yelled at him, but with tears coming down my face. He didn't stop, instead he firmly grabbed me and started to kiss me passionately. I wanted him to stop, but for some reason my lips didn't. They welcomed his tongue in and I massaged it with mine. I felt his hands on face as he turned my head to his liking as he continued to massage my tongue with his. His kiss was almost as if he had me paralyzed because I kept telling myself over and over to push him away, but my arms wouldn't move. Finally, I was able to get him off of me as I felt him get hard. "Follow me." I told him as I got in my car. He didn't hesitate nor did he ask questions. I wanted Keith more than ever now and I needed him. Zavier was gone and I don't think that he was ever coming back. I was starting to think that maybe somehow he found out about me and Keith and he left or maybe he didn't, but I knew that he wasn't there.

I don't know how fast we were driving, but before I knew it we were in the elevator trying to take each other clothes off. "Make love to me, Keith." I told him as he kissed me on my neck. "I want you. I want you so bad." He told me as he started kissing me. "I want you, now. Now!" I shouted and kissed him back. "I love you." He whispered in my ear as the doors opened. "Excuse me, are you Ms. Thomas?" A short, stocky, black man questioned me as the elevator doors opened. "Why? Yes I am. Is there something that I can help you with?" I said to this strange man as I knew that he was probably there to serve me papers. "I do apologize for showing up like this and I had just left my card on your door" He said. "Sir? I'm sorry but, I don't mean to be rude and all. But, who in the hell are you and why are you here?" I asked. Keith had placed his hand around my waist letting me know to calm down. But, this man was just talking and I have yet to know who he was and why he was interrupting me from letting Keith blow my back out. Hell, that's what was really pissing me off. "Again, I apologize. I'm Detective Rogers. Is there some place that we can speak more privately?" He asked me as he pointed into the direction of my hotel room. I nodded my head and lead the way.

The only thing I could think of was, what kind of client was I getting now or what kind of information they needed from me for a client if I this was a subpoena. "Hey, I'm just gonna go and you can call me later." Keith said as he stood in the doorway. "Like, hell. You're gonna come in, too. He might now even be a real detective. Don't you dare leave me alone with this strange man. Remember what happen when I was alone last time?" I told Keith as I placed my hand on my hip. I didn't care that the detective heard me because I was speaking the truth. For all I knew he could have been someone that Eric hired to kill me and no one would know who did it and why. "I take it you don't like the law?" The detective asked. "No, I don't trust strangers." I told him. "Well, I can understand that." He said as he took out his notepad and pen. "So, obviously you busy so I'll get right to it." He said smartly. "Now, what does that supposed to mean?" I asked as I crossed my legs. Keith placed his hand on my shoulder to remind me again to keep calm, but this detective was pissing me off. "Nothing, Ms. Thomas I know that you are the CEO, at one of the top Law Firms so I just know that you're busy." He said as he was writing. I rolled my eyes at him because the entire time he was focused on the contact between me and Keith. "Ms. Thomas, can you tell me how do you know Mr. Zavier Price?" The detective asked me. I couldn't respond at first because the fact that a detective was asking me a question about someone who I completely shut off was scary. "Yes, we were engaged." I told him. "Were? So, you guys broke up? Did he break up with you or did you break up with him? Are you okay with talking in front of him?" He interrogated. "I don't know. We had a fight, but made up and then we had a small argument. I tried calling him ever since and he hasn't returned my phone calls and he hasn't responded to my texts, so I just assumed that left me. Yes, I want Keith to stay because like I said I don't trust strangers. Plus,

I'm a lawyer and it's always good to have a second pair of ears whenever you're talking to the law." I told him as my eyes started to water up. Keith immediately wrapped his arm around me. "Smart. So, you haven't heard from him for almost a week now and didn't report it to the police?" The detective asked me. "Huh? What? Why would I report our breakup to the police?" I asked him. "So, is this your boyfriend?" He asked me as he was writing. "No, Keith is a close friend and why would I report my personal business to the police? Our issues is none of your business." I responded to the detective. "What kind of issues, Ms. Thomas?" The detective asked. I ignored him because I refused to tell this man that I was cheating on Zavier with Keith. I didn't need the entire town knowing my business. "Ms. Thomas, if you refuse to answer my question here I'm afraid that I will be forced to take you in." He sat up. "Kait, just answer his question." Keith said as he looked at me with fear in his eyes after he heard what the detective said. "What do you wanna know?" I asked followed by a deep sigh. "Well, for starters you can tell me the truth about you and this man here. What did you say his name was again?" Detective Rogers asked and pointed to Keith. "Don't say a word. " I told Keith as I looked at the Detective. I then proceeded to ask the Detective numerous of questions as to why he needed to know his name. After he couldn't give me a good enough answer I told him to direct all of his questions to me. "I see why you win all of your cases. Well, something told me to write down his name, but I will remember it." He said with a laugh. I asked him if he could hurry this up because I still didn't know what this had to do with me and Zavier breaking up. "The bottom line, Ms. Thomas, is that there is something that you're not telling me." The detective said as he eyed me and Keith. "Like what?" I told the detective as I folded my arms. "Like, after not hearing from Mr. Price why didn't you report it to the police?" He stated. "I told you. Our business is none of your business. Our issues is private. I don't want the entire......." I said, but the detective interrupted. "See, Ms. Thomas. None of that makes sense and none of that is true. You didn't report because you know exactly what happen and you know exactly what was going on?" Detective Rogers said as he pointed his pen at me. I was looked on in shock and thinking like well, he is a detective so it is possible for him to find out about me and Keith sleeping around, but I wasn't gonna come out and just say it. "Well, he deserved it." I told the detective as I sat back. "Wow? You are one sick woman." Detective Rogers said as he shook his head. "Hey, watch your mouth." Keith said as he stood up. "Calm down." I consoled Keith as I stood up in front of him. "You better get yourself a good lawyer." He told me. "Lawyer? For what?" I asked him. "Murder." He said. "Who said anything about killing anybody?" I asked him. "You did!" Detective Rogers shouted out as he pointed his pen at me again. "I didn't said I killed someone. Nobody is dead. What the hell are you talking about?" I told him as I held my hands out with confusion. "You said he deserved it." He said as he read out loud from his notepad of repeating my statement. "Yes, I was referring to being cheating on. Zavier deserved to be cheated on." I told him as I nodded my head. "Now, this murder thing. You lost me, what is this murder thing you're talking about?" I interrogated him this time. "You mean you don't know?" He asked me with a confused expression on his face. "Know what?" I asked him as I glanced over at Keith. "Ms. Thomas, tell me where were you about a week ago?" He asked me as he took out his notepad again. "I was in California visiting with friends." I told him. He then told me that he was going to check with the airlines to validate my traveling dates and proceeded to leave. "Wait! Wait! Hold on, nothing you just said made sense to me. You came here interrupting me and ruining my day. Then, you went from talking about nothing to something and that went from cheating to murder. From there you said that I murdered Zavier and asked me about where I've been for a week. Nothing that you just said is making sense to me right now. Can you just explain to me what does Zavier..." I paused as I saw Zavier's picture pop up on the TV because I remember leaving it on before I left this morning. "Turn it up." I told Keith. "Tonight at 9. There is still no news as to what happened to Dr. Zavier Price. Police are still investigating on whether it was suicide or a crime of passion." The reporter said. "We do not have any suspects..." Keith immediately turned the TV before the Chief of police could finish his sentence. "I'll let myself out." Detective Rogers said as he noticed how quiet I was. I closed the door behind him and felt my legs getting weak. My body became numb and I could feel myself sliding down, but Keith caught me before

I hit the floor. "Shh....it's okay." He said as he held me. "It's not true. Is it? Did I do this? Yeah, I did!" I shouted out at Keith with tears falling down my face. "No, you didn't do anything wrong. Stop it." He said as he was wiping my eyes. "I did kill him. I did! I really did. He found out about us and killed himself. It's my fault! It's all my fault! Oh God!" I screamed out when I realized what I just heard. Zavier was dead and it was all because of me.

There was no other explanation as to why he would kill himself except for finding out about me and Keith. "He's dead! He's dead! No! No! No! No!" I kept screamed over and over as Keith held me. I was waiting for Zavier to pop out the closet just to say that he was kidding in order to catch me cheating, but he never did. "Shh...baby. Try to calm down." Keith said as he picked me up and carried me to the couch. "I killed him. It's my fault. Keith, I killed him." I told him as he kept trying to get me to calm down. "You didn't kill him, Kait so stop saying that." Keith admonished. "How do you know that?" I asked him as I tried catching my breath. "Because for whatever reason he did what he did to himself wasn't because of you, okay? You are so loving and caring and if he wanted to be mad at anybody he would be mad at me and not you, but there's has to be another explanation." Keith said as he got up to get the door. "Tell them to go away." I instructed as I got up to go to the bedroom because I didn't want whomever it was to see me like this. It probably was the housekeeper bringing more towels because nobody knew that I was here. I could hear Keith talking to a man at the door, but I didn't run to go see because for one I looked a mess, and for two, I knew that he could handle himself. "Are you serious right now?" I heard Keith yell. I could barely hear what the other man was saying, but whatever he said pissed Keith off because he slammed the door in the man's face. "Who was it?" I asked. Keith was silent as he walked into the bedroom with his hands on his head. "Keith?" I said as I looked at him waiting for him to tell me who was at the door and why he looked like he was ready to whoop somebody's ass. "Let's talk about it tomorrow." He told me as he sat on the bed and tried to kiss me on the forehead. "No, we're gonna talk about it now." I told him as I pushed him away. "I don't wanna get you back upset. Because you see how calm you are right now." He told me as he tried to hold my hand, but I pulled it away. "You not telling me what's going on is gonna make me upset." I told him as I got up and paced the room. Keith laid back on the bed and covered his face and took a deep breath. He knew that he didn't have any other choice, but to tell me otherwise I was gonna become a bitch from hell. "So?" I said with my arms folded as I sat on the desk in the bedroom. "That was the Detective Rogers." Keith said. I let out a loud breath and rolled my eyes when I heard Keith say his name. "What did his ugly ass want?" "Well? Two things. He gonna check to make sure you were out of town because he thinks that you really were the one that killed Zavier. And he wants you to identify the body." Keith said as he got up to come stand in front of me. I placed my finger on my chin and stared at the ceiling for a minute. "Kait?

Kait? Babe, you okay?" Keith asked as he snapped his fingers. "Oh, yeah. I was just wondering how much Eric spent and how long had he been working on this. I mean, if Zavier is in on it, okay whatever, but why? That's what I need to find out." I said as I got down and went into the kitchen to open my laptop. "What are you doing?" Keith asked me. "I'm going to hire a private investigator. If this is how Eric wanna play, then I can play dirty, too." I began typing. Keith slapped my laptop shut and pushed it away. "What the hell are you doing?" I asked him as I held my hand up. "Are you even listening?" Keith asked as he pointed to his ears.

I didn't know why Keith was so upset because all of this was made up. "It's not true. It's not! This is something that Eric has come up with in order to get me to lose my mind so that I would end up back in that damn crazy house. But, it's not gonna work. I'm gonna stay calm." I told Keith. "Baby, I know that you're upset right now. Okay? But, I don't think that this is a lie." Keith told me as he rubbed both of my arms. "You're not listening to me right now! Eric is a bastard, okay? He is capable of anything." I informed Keith. "Kaitlyn, you're upset and I know that you don't want to believe this, but I don't think that this is a lie. I know the things that Eric has done to you is unforgivable, but do you really think that he would go through all this trouble to hurt you even more?" Keith tried to convince me. "Yes, because that is the type of bastard he is. He's evil and he doesn't care about nobody but himself." "Besides what makes you think that this isn't a joke and its's real?" I asked Keith. He was silent for a minute and turned around. "What is it?" I asked Keith as I turned in his direction, but he turned again. "Keith! Keith!" I yelled as I was in his face, but he kept turning his head. "Baby, I'm sorry." He said as a tear fell out of his eye. "What? I don't understand? What do you mean by that?" I asked him as I wiped his tear away. "I thought the same thing that maybe Eric was being cruel and hired a fake detective, but then he showed me." Keith paused as he looked into my eyes and held me. "Showed you what?" I yelled at him. "He showed me the pictures. Baby, it's him. I wouldn't lie to you and that's why I am sorry because it's true." He told me as he immediately held me. I didn't react at first because the words didn't make sense at first until I recapped from the beginning to now. "No! No! Zavier!" I shouted out as I tried to get out of Keith's arms. "I don't wanna live anymore! I don't wanna live!" I yelled as I struggled with him. "Shh...Baby, it's not your fault. Don't talk like that I need you." Keith said as he was still holding on to me tight. "I'm gonna be sick." I said as I was still sobbing. He let me go and I quickly ran to the bathroom and slammed the door. But, he immediately ran after me and told me to open the door. I refused to as I was rambling through the cabinets looking for something. Something that would take away this pain. I hated my life and didn't want to hurt anymore. Zavier was gone, well at least that's what I was told. "Kait, open the door." Keith shouted as he was banging on it. I was quiet, but I was still rambling until I found what I needed. "What is that? Kait! Kait! Dammit!" Keith shouted as he kicked the door in. "No!" Keith yelled as he saw a prescribed bottle on the floor and the pills in my hand. I had darted pass him and ran into the kitchen to take them. I thought I ran fast enough, but apparently not because Keith had his hands on my mouth squeezing my cheeks together. "Spit it out! Spit it out!" He shouted out as he held my head over the sink. "Kait, baby please, spit them out!" Keith commanded as he was still trying to get me to spit the pills out. I think he felt me swallow a few because what he did next was unthinkable. He held me down and forced my mouth open and stuck his finger down my throat in order to make me throw up. I tried to squirm and move, but he was too strong and I was exhausted from fighting against him. He was able to get me to throw up twice and I was mad. I could tell that I wore him out because he had taken his shirt off to wipe his face. "Yes, I have someone who just took maybe about four or five pills of Ativan. They were able to vomit twice. Okay, okay. Thank you." Keith said. I rolled over to look at wall because I got tired of smelling my vomit. I just didn't understand how my life went from being wonderful to crap within month. "I called to speak with a nurse at the hospital. Don't worry I didn't give them your name. She said that you should be okay, but that I would need to keep a watch on you for twenty four hours." He reached down to pick me up. "C'mon I got you a hot bubble bath running." He said as carried me to the bathroom. I heard everything that Keith was saying, but all I could think was that he was going to be next. He was going to leave me too.

I tried waiting a day or two before identifying the body, but I couldn't take it anymore. I had to know for sure whether or not if Zavier was really dead or if he had just left as Alivia had told me. "I don't think....." Keith began to say, but I interrupted him by putting my hand up. "Don't!" I told him as we were pulling up at the hospital. Even though he took care of me last night I was still upset with him; therefore he didn't have the right to speak to me at this point.

As we were getting out, I could tell Keith was worried about me and that he didn't want me to do this right now, but I had to know. "Excuse me? Where is your coroner's office?" I asked the receptionist. "Go down this hall. You'll see the elevators. Push the button that says level B and not basement. Otherwise, you'll be in the garage." The receptionist ordered. I thanked her as me and Keith went into the direction she told us. "You're not ready. Look, you're shaking." Keith said as he held my hand. "I'm fine. Eventually, I was gonna have to come and do this and why are you even touching me? Why are you talking to me?" He didn't respond, but proceeded to kiss me. I hated him when he knew what to do without me telling him to do it. "I love you." He said as the elevator stopped. We saw a man sitting at a desk and notified him that we were there to identify the body of Zavier Price. He instructed us to go up the stairs and wait in a room and when he located the deceased, he would then pull the curtain back. I was scared and nervous at the same time, but I was glad that Keith was there to support me. "See, its taking him too long. Maybe I was right. Zavier probably....." I paused as I noticed the curtain slowly moving. "Breath...breath." Keith coached me as I immediately grabbed his shirt when the curtains became wider. "Ma'am, can you please identify the decease?" The coroner instructed. I got up and placed both of my hands on the glass and nodded yes. "Ma'am, I'm sorry, but can you please state the deceased name?" He ordered again. "Yes! It's Zavier!" I yelled out as tears ran down my face and fell to the floor. "Yes!" I yelled out again. I saw Keith fanning his hand, but I didn't know what he was doing until I saw the curtains move again. "No! No! No!" I screamed as the curtain closed. "Zavier! Zavier!" I screamed out as I was banging on the glass window. "Kaitlyn, stop. You don't need to look at him like that, okay?" Keith told me as he pulled me away from the glass window. "Zavier!" I screamed out again as Keith dragged me out of the room. "I wanna see him! I wanna see him!" I yelled at the coroner as I saw him coming out of the room where Zavier laid. "Um, we've stopped letting family members do that as you can see." The coroner said as he pointed to the room that we were just in. "I don't give a damn about that! I want to see him! Move!" I told him as I pushed and made my way in. I couldn't believe what I was seeing as I saw the love of my life laying on that table. "This isn't real. This isn't real. I'm gonna wake up and find you lying next to me, right? Yeah, this is just a bad dream." I told him as I reached to rub his head. "You can't touch him, ma'am. Especially without gloves. The police are still investigating." The coroner said. "Kaitlyn, you gonna get this man fired. Let's go." Keith told gently pulled me away. "It's not real. I'm not here. You're not here. He's not here." I said as I pointed to each of us individually. "We can go back to my house if you like, if you don't feel like being around any people." Keith said. "I don't care." I told him. "Kaitlyn, I don't know what to say to you right now. But, don't shut me out. I'm here for you and I love you. Please, right now just don't shut me out." Keith pleaded with me. "I'm not. I just don't feel like talking right now." I told him as we left the hospital. It never fails. Once I'm happy something comes in and knocks me on my ass. I usually got up, but this time I can barely breathe in order to get myself back up.

CHAPTER 22

I called Stan and told him what happened. He asked where I was and I told him that I was with Keith. "Well, I don't know him all that well, but I'm glad you're not alone." Stan said.

"I don't....I can't....how...." I kept trying to get my words together as I was trying to understand why this happened. "Hey, hey. It's okay." Stan told me as he heard my voice trembling. "No, it's not, but it will be." I told him as I wiped my eyes. "Kait? Where does Keith live?" Stan asked me. "Why? You getting jealous, again?" I asked him. "No, cause I wanna be there for my friend. I can't come tomorrow, but maybe the day after." He told me. I told Stan how to get to Keith's house and he knew exactly where he lived. "So, once I pass your job I just keep straight pass Courts Avenue and then I make a left and keep straight until I get to a yield sign and then make a right on Allison street and his house is the last house on the left?" He asked me again. "Yes, or I can give you the address and you can put it in your navigation system." I told him as I laughed. He laughed, too, as he forgot that there was an easier way. "I'll text it to you." I told him as I stood up. "Okay, get some rest. I love you, baby girl." He said. "I love you too, Stan." I replied as we hung up. Stan always could make me laugh whenever I was having a bad day and I loved him for that.

I walked downstairs to see if Keith was still there and he was. "Hi." I said as I made my way down the stairs. "Hi, back." He said with a smile. "Thank you." I told him as I sat down on the couch with him. "For, what?" He asked me. "For letting me stay here, like this. I gotta admit being here is better than being at the hotel with all that noise." I told him. "Well, I just want you to be comfortable with everything that has happened to you and like now. I mean, you deserve..." Keith stopped as he saw my eyes watering up. "I'm sorry." He said as he pulled me into his chest. "No, it's fine. I need to accept the fact that he's gone and that he's never coming back." I blurted out as tears started rolling down my face. Keith held me tighter and told me to let it out. "I'm here for you and I'm not going anywhere." Keith told me. "Kiss me." I told him as I wiped my tears from my cheeks. "What?" Keith questioned my mentality. "I want you...to...kiss me and...to make love to me." I said as I kissed his neck. I could tell it was turning him on as he got comfortable with his hands rubbing my ass. "Are you sure you wanna do this?" He asked me. I didn't say anything. I only went in to kiss his lips some more. I heard him moaning as the kiss became more intimate. I pulled his shirt over his head and moved my hands down to his pants to unbutton them. "I want you!" I whispered in his ear. We switched positons as he picked me up and laid me on the couch. I began to moan as he kissed me on my neck and squeezed my breasts.

For a moment it was feeling good until the doorbell rang. "Don't get it." I told him as I pulled him back as he got up to answer. He stayed until they rung the bell three times back to back. "Are you expecting anyone?" I asked him. "No, it's probably my neighbor. I'll get rid of them. Don't move." He told me as he kissed me before getting up to answer the door.

It didn't take too long, because before I knew anything I heard Keith yelling my name and asking me if I was descent. "What's wrong?" I asked Keith as he walked in the den slowly. "Hello, again Ms. Thomas. We are going to have to stop meeting up like this." Detective Rogers said. "What are you doing here?" I asked him. "Me? I'm doing my job which is solving crimes. On the other hand I should be asking you the same question?" Detective Rogers said. "Watch it?" Keith said as he stood in front of me to defend me. "No, I got it. As a lawyer Detective Rogers, I would advise you to tread likely because slander of one's name is a crime you know." I gently reminded him as I pushed Keith to the side. "Oh, yes ma'am I do know that. But, do you know murder is crime, too?" The detective sat down. I placed my hand on my forehead because here he was again talking in riddles and I didn't have time for it. "How long have you two been dating?" He asked me and Keith. "We just started....." Keith started to say, but I interrupted him to ask the Detective what my personal life had to do with him finding out what happened to Zavier. "Well, you see. Mr. Price suffered from one gunshot wound to the heart. It was at close range. So whoever did this was someone that he knew. Now, on the night of his murder Ms. Thomas you were in California so I know you didn't do it, but Mr. Palmerson? Where were you?" The detective inquired. "Don't say a word. I will have you to know that Keith doesn't know Zavier at all. They have maybe seen each other twice, so there is no way that he could be involved. So, unless you have evidence against him I suggest you leave." I told the Detective as I got up and pointed to the door. "Man, it must pay off to be screwing a lawyer." He said as he got up. "What!" Keith said as he got up. "Keith! He's trying to get a reason to take you to jail to talk to you alone without a lawyer. Let it go." I said as I placed my hands on his chest to push him back. "He was right, you're very smart." Detective Rogers said as he walked to the door. "Excuse me?" I said as I turned around. "Your dad, I mean your uncle. Eric? Yeah, I know everything, Ms. Thomas." He said as he opened the door. "Well, obviously you don't if you're here." I told him as he walked outside. "Don't worry Ms. Thomas I always get my man or woman. It doesn't matter to me. I always win. Y'all enjoy the rest of your day." He saluted us he got into his car.

"Are you okay?" Keith asked me as he closed the door. "I need to be alone right now." I told Keith as I went into the kitchen. I searched the cabinets until I had found my favorite drink, tequila. She always made me feel better. "You're not okay?" Keith questioned. "Keith, dammit no! Would you be okay? Ask yourself that." I remarked to him as I poured me another glass of tequila. "I'm sorry. I can't imagine what you're feeling right now. Tell me what can I do to make this feel better?" Keith said as he kissed my forehead. "I'm gonna take me a long hot bubble bath and then come back downstairs so that we can finish what we started." I told Keith as I kissed him. "So, you just gonna take my entire bottle?" Keith asked. "Yep, I perform better when I'm highly intoxicated." I told him with a smile. "We can finish right now." He said as he started kissing my neck. I pushed him away and told him that I really just needed some alone time and he understood, but really I was lying to Keith.

I had other thoughts in my mind and had come to a realization that my life wasn't going to get better. There was no hope for me in this world anymore and no matter how hard I tried to look at the bright side there wasn't one. People who said they loved me had betrayed and hurt me the most. I don't know how I could of let all of this happen and why did I continue to let it happen. I was pathetic, weak and blind to the eye because of my heart trying to love and be open. So, I refuse to take it anymore. No one would miss me and no one would care. "Do you need anything?" I heard Keith yelled up the stairs. "No, I'm fine." I yelled back down as I quickly swallowed a handful of Ativan that was prescribed for me when I was attacked and washed it down with a full bottle of tequila. I sat on the cold bathroom floor just staring at the wall and thinking about my life. It was fading and fading until I could see no more light.

Keith was heading up the stairs to check on Kaitlyn until he heard the doorbell ring. "Hey?" Keith said as he saw Stan standing at the door. "Hi. Kait here?" Stan asked. "Yeah, she's upstairs. She told me that you're weren't coming until tomorrow." Keith told

Stan as he motioned for him to come in. "Yeah, I was, but something she said didn't sit right with me." Stan told Keith. "Well, I've been watching her closely and she seems okay. I mean you can tell that she's not fine, but she's gonna be okay." Keith told him. "Where is she right, now?" Stan asked. "She's upstairs taking a bath." Keith told him. "Did she say anything weird or do anything strange before she went upstairs?" Stan asked. "Nope, she said she just wanted to relax and take a hot bath and uh....oh she did take my entire bottle of tequila up there with her." Keith said with a smirk. Stan was silent and jumped up to go look for Kaitlyn. "Kait? Kait? Where man?" Stan yelled at Keith. "Right there. The second door on your left." Keith said "Kait? Kait?" Stan said as he knocked on the door. "It's locked. You got a key?" Stan asked Keith. "No. Kaitlyn? Open the door. We just wanna make sure that you're okay. Kaitlyn? Look....." Keith said as he pointed to the water running down under the door. Stan told Keith to move back as he was going to bust the door down. With his athletic skills he was successful on the first try. "Oh my God!" Keith said as he saw Kaitlyn's lifeless body on the bathroom floor. Keith immediately turned the water off as it had Kaitlyn soaked. "Wake up! Kait, baby please wake up!" Stan was yelling as he shook Kaitlyn. "I need an ambulance please! Hurry up! I don't know...I don't know. Stan what did she take?" Keith asked Stan as he was on the phone with the 911 operator. Stan looked around her to see if he could find out what Kaitlyn had taken. "Uhh....a bottle of tequila and.....OH MY GOD! This entire bottle of Ativan." He yelled out as he rubbed his bald head. Keith continued to talk to the 911 operator explaining the current situation while Stan tried to revive the love of his life. "You can't die on me. Do you hear me? I love you.....I love you! I've loved you ever since I first laid eyes on you with that beautiful smile. I wished I would of told you sooner and not like this. You have to wake up because you gotta fuss and cuss me out about how I feel about you, okay? So, you can't go...not now. GOD PLEASE! HELP!" Stan was crying and screaming out hoping that God will forgive Kaitlyn of this and send her back to him.

As the ambulance came in, they asked Keith and Stan to move back in order for them to evaluate Kaitlyn. "Okay, I got a pulse but it's very faint. I say we got twenty minutes to get her pumped before it's too late." An EMT noted. With oxygen on Kaitlyn, the EMT asked who was going to ride on the ambulance as Stan got in. He heard the driver do a code blue over the radio to the ER informing them that they had a very critical condition. "They're gonna take good care of you. Okay? Stay with me because I can't live without you. I would take advantage of you, but I don't think right now is a good time." Stan said to her and hoped that she would open her eyes to hear him being so ignorant. Keith got in his car behind the ambulance with his flashers on and prayed to God to please save Kaitlyn.

When my eyes finally opened, I was in Eric's house and didn't know what I was doing there because I remembered being in Stan's house. "Hello, Kaitlyn." A tall lean man said to me. "Who are you?" I said to him as I turned around to see this elderly man. "I'm Eric Sr., your grandfather." He said as he walked towards me. "I don't understand. Is this hell? This gotta be hell." I said as I looked around for a red man with a pitch fork. "No, sweetheart this isn't hell and no you're not dead. You're in a dream of your depressed memory and I am one of them. You don't remember me, do you?" He asked me. I told him not really and asked him why I was here at Eric's house. "Well, for starters you really didn't want to kill yourself. He saw it in your heart." Eric Sr. said as he pointed to the sky. "You felt like ending your life would help you forget about all the wrong that has happened to you, but guess what baby girl? You're stronger then you know. You whole power within yourself that if you only believe then you shall conquer." He assured me. I was silent as I was trying to figure out this life or dimension that I was in. "Haven't you ever wondered why Eric was determined to make your life a living hell and to drive you insane? It's because you have something that he wants and needs." He said as he placed his hand on my shoulder. A flood of memories starting flashing before my eyes of him when he placed his hand on my shoulder and I immediately jumped up to hug him. "Grandpa E!" I screamed with tears of joy coming down my face. "Yes, I remember everything. Why couldn't I remember it before?" I asked him. "Well, sometimes you have to bring the good with the bad. Case in point, me at Eric Jr. house where it all started. Now, we don't have much time. Listen close and listen good. You hold the key to what is written." He told me as a light started shining through the windows. "What does that even mean?" I asked him. "Trust your heart and believe in yourself. I will always be there whenever you need me. I love you baby girl." He said to me as he turned towards the light. I had to admit that this was creeping me out a little and not really knowing exactly where I was didn't help at all.

As I kept thinking over and over about what he meant that I had the key, I saw a fog of smoke coming through the kitchen door. I didn't know what was coming so I got up and ran to the front door only to be pulled by a gust of wind. The wind was so strong that it sucked the rug right from up under me. I grab the door frame and held on as tight as I could, but I heard a voice telling me to let go and at that moment I trusted myself as my grandpa E said. "Alright, I got a strong pulse. Turn the oxygen up and let's get a heart monitor on. Stat!" The doctor yelled as Kaitlyn had lost consciousness after having her stomach pumped. Stan saw the doctor coming out of the ER operating room and asked if Kaitlyn was going to be okay. "We had a little bit of a scare, but she's gonna be fine." The doctor informed Keith and Stan. They were both relieved to know that their friend was going to be okay; however, Keith had no idea that Stan was in love with Kaitlyn, too. "That's good to hear, right." Keith said to Stan. "Yeah it is. I'm gonna make a phone call." He told Keith as he walked away. Keith just nodded his head and sat down in the waiting room. The situation was awkward because here it was, two men loving one woman and neither one was willing to back off.

"Well, well isn't this interesting." Eric noted as he walked in. "Excuse me?" Keith said as he saw his mother and Eric walking into the waiting area. "Don't play crazy with me boy. I know exactly who you are." Eric reminded him. "I'm sorry, sir, I think that you have me confused with someone else." He told him. Cassandra was silent because no one could ever find out the truth about her and Keith. "Why are ya'll here?" Stan asked as he walked back into the waiting area. "Well, she is my niece and whenever something like this happens they call the next of kin. I think it's time to make that call again." Eric said as he reached for his phone. Stan immediately charged at Eric and had him at the collar and pushed him against the wall. "Like hell, you are." He told Eric. "Hey, man this isn't the time or place." Keith told him as he tried to get Stan to put Eric down. "You should listen to your friend here. What's your name, son?" Eric said with a smirk. "Gentlemen, do I have to call security?" The doctor said as he walked in. "No." Stan said as he let go of Eric. "When can I see my daughter?" Cassandra asked. "Well, she's very weak right now and we want her to save her strength, so we're trying to let her rest. But, she's asking for you." The doctor said as he pointed to Stan. Keith was disappointed, but he refused to leave the hospital because he wanted Kaitlyn to know that he was a man of his word. He wanted her to know that he was gonna be there for her no matter what. "So, can I see her?" Stan asked the doctor. "Yes, but please. Do say or do anything to upset her." The doctor said as he asked Stan to follow him. "Don't worry I'm not gonna have her committed. Besides if I do that, then neither one of us will get the money. You just make sure that you do a better job than that Zavier. Fooling with that damn woman got his ass killed." Eric said to Keith as he watched Stan leave.

Stan was nervous about seeing Kaitlyn. He didn't know why she wanted to see him and not Keith, but he didn't care. He was just glad that she asked for him which meant that she cared and possibly loved him. "Are you awake?" Stan whispered as he walked in. I motioned for him to come sit beside me, but he sat in the chair next to me instead. "Shh...don't try to speak. The doctor said that you need to get some rest." Stan told me as he saw that I was trying to talk. "I'm ....soo...rrr...yy..." I whimpered out as he held my hand. "Shhh....don't talk. Why are you so hard headed?" He said as he began to rub my head. I couldn't stay awake for more than five minutes at a time, but I could hear Stan telling me that he wasn't leaving my side and that made me feel safe.

CHAPTER 23

After four days of hospitalization, I was ready to finally go home. It was required that I be put on watch in case I decided to attempt suicide again, but after my past life or epiphany experience, I don't plan on ever doing that anytime soon. I guess you can say that it was a wake up call letting me know that God still loves me and he has never forsaken me. I was too focused on the negativity in my life that I couldn't focus on the good and enjoy the people who have always been there. I had Stan and Alivia who have been there for me whenever I needed them and they always told the truth even when I didn't want to hear it. That's when I realized that I had people who really cared for me and that was worth living for. "Are you all set?" Stan asked as he entered my room. "Stan, listen I need to talk to you." I said as I was getting my stuff together. "Hey, babe I'm gonna get the car........" Keith said as he paused and saw Stan in the room. "Hey, man." Keith said as he reached out to shake Stan's hand, but instead Stan gave him a nod. "I'll grab this and meet you out front." Keith grabbed my bag and kissed me. "I tried calling you, but you wouldn't answer." I told Stan. "I left my phone at home, but

I had just assumed that I would be...you know what forget it. It's fine." Stan he folded his arms. "See? This is what I am talking about." I told him as I sat on the edge of the hospital bed. "See what? What am I looking at?" Stan said. I hated it when he got into his moods because that meant that everything that came out of his mouth was going to be smart. "Sit down." I told him as I patted the other side of the bed. "I heard everything that you said to me and I know how you feel about me, but I don't feel the same way. I tried and it's just not there. To me that would be unfair if I was just with you because I knew how you felt and knowing I didn't feel the same. Our friendship is too important for me to ruin that and I do love you just not in that way." I him stated as I rubbed his back. "Well, I can respect that, but is it fair to Keith?" He asked. "Keith and I are different. I can see myself in a relationship with Keith. I'm not gonna say that I am all head over heels in love with him like I was with Zavier because that takes time. However, I will say that there is something there. I just gotta figure out what it is." I told him as I got up to make sure that I wasn't leaving anything. "I can't do anything, but respect that and just know that if he hurts you he has to answer to me." Stan said as he hugged me. I didn't doubt that after Keith told me how Stan busted the door down I'm pretty sure he didn't want to answer to him. I was glad that we were on good terms and that my life was trying to get back to normal, but there still was a few things that I had to take care of before I moved on with Keith and that was burying the love of my life and completely cutting all ties off with the Thomas family.

It wasn't my plan nor idea to be with Keith at the time, but it happened. I don't know what we had or how things were going to happen between us, but the feelings were there. Besides he has always been there whenever I needed him and not questioning nor judging my actions. "You know you can always come move in with me right." Keith said as he sat down on the bed of my hotel room. "I know, but I want to take things slow and one day at time." I told him. "Stan didn't look to happy the other day about us? I believe he has a crush on you." He insisted. I told him that Stan did liked me, but I just didn't see him in that way like he wanted me too.

As I was looking over the obituary for Zavier's funeral tomorrow, I became emotional. My guilty conscience was getting the best of me because here I was in a hotel with another man, and tomorrow I was burying the love of my life. "Hey, hey. Come here." Keith said as he saw me covering my eyes. "This is wrong. This is so wrong." I told him as he held me. "Baby, listen to me. You have nothing to be guilty about nor have you done anything wrong. You said it yourself that you thought that he just abandoned you because you haven't heard from him in days. How could you have known that something like this happened?" Keith said as he wiped my eyes. He was right in a way. I shouldn't feel bad because no one ever thinks the worst about any situation especially death, but I couldn't help it. "Do you think that he would want you to feel sad or be happy?" Keith asked me. I had to think about it for a minute because when me and Zavier last spoke we were supposed to be happy together. I wasn't imagining my life with anyone else. "I guess he would want me to be happy." I told Keith as I tried to force a smile. He kissed me trying to get my mind off of it for a while and it worked. "What are you doing?" I asked him as he started kissing my neck. "Nothing. I'm smelling it. It smells good." He said. "With your tongue?" I asked him as he was kissing my neck. He didn't say anything as he continued to kiss my neck. I could tell already that he was learning how to get my mind off of things and that was going to take him a long way. "Don't get it." He told me when he heard my phone ring. I started not too, but it kept ringing back to back. "Hello?" I answered with a giggle as Keith was blowing in my ear. "Damn, you sure sound happy for someone who's about to bury their fiancée' tomorrow." Alivia said. "No, I was watching something on TV." I told her as I pushed Keith back. "Well, I was calling to tell you that I made it in. Do you want me to come to Stan's house?" She asked. "I'm not there." I told her. "Okay? Are you at Zavier's house?" She asked. "Nope." I responded. "Okay? So, where the hell are you?" She asked me. I told her that I was staying at a hotel and she asked where. I knew she wanted to be with me to show support, but I had Keith there. "I just need some alone time at the moment, if that's okay?" I told her as I sat back down on the bed. I could tell that she was pissed when she got off the phone with me. "Does she know about us?" Keith asked as he pointed to the phone. "Nope, but she will now. She's headed over to Stan's house and because he doesn't like you he's gonna tell her." I told him as I lean back against the headboard. "So is that a good thing or a bad thing?" He asked me a he laid on my chest. "Well, considering the fact that she knew I liked you all along. The only thing that she will tell me is that she told me so." I said as I rubbed his head. He looked up at me with a smile and tried to kiss me, but instead I pushed him back. "Really?" He asked me. "Yep, I don't like you." I told him as I hit him in the head with the pillow. "I know you love me." He said as he threw the pillow back. We were officially having a pillow fight which had us chasing each other around the room. "Get back." I told Keith as he was coming towards me. "Say you give up." He said. "No." I said with a laugh as he was tickled me. "Stop...stop.....stop. Baby, you win. You win." I told him as he was still tickling me and we fell on the floor. "That's right. I love you, baby." He said as he kissed me.

Even though Keith would say that he loved me and I never said it back it never bothered him. I was glad that he felt comfortable to say it when he was ready and not force me to say it just because he was saying it. "I want you right now, baby." He whispered in my ear. "Me too, but you know what the doctor said." I remind him as the doctor told me as I needed to keep my stress level to a minimal. "I know, but I think that this will make you feel good." He said as he lift my shirt up to kiss my stomach. I tried to resist, but me and Keith sexual attraction was always high whenever we were around each other. "Baby, we can't." I whimpered out as Keith was kissing my inner thigh.

He was still silent and still kissing my thighs working his way on down. I knew where he was going and yet I really didn't try to stop him. "Baby? Baby? Keith?" I whispered as he made his way to his final destination. I felt his tongue going in and out and his hands under my ass gripping my cheeks. He knew what he was doing and I did too. I placed my hands on his head as he had placed an arch in my back because it was feeling so good. "Aww...Keith. That feels so good. Don't stop." I told him as he placed a finger inside and was licking me the same time. I cracked my eyes open for a second to take a peak just to see. "So, this is how you do me?" Zavier said as he leaned over me. I screamed so loud that I think I hit a note louder then Mariah Carey. "Baby, what's wrong?" Keith asked. I couldn't say anything as I wrapped myself up in the bedsheet. "Kaitlyn, you're shaking. What's wrong?" Keith asked. I still couldn't respond. The only I could do was rock back and forth and think about what I just saw. I know it was only my imagination, but for what reason. "I...I.....I...I need to get some sleep." I told him as I laid down. "Okay? Do you wanna talk about what just happened?" Keith asked me. I begged him to please let it go and I promised him that I would tell him later. He agreed and didn't bothered me about it again. I was glad that Keith wasn't like Stan in that way. He didn't keep asking you what was wrong over and over again until you told him. "Will you hold me?" I asked Keith. "Of course." Keith said as he cuddled in the bed with me. I wasn't scared to be alone. I just wanted to be held and needed comfort in order to be prepared for the next day.

I had an hour before it was time for the funeral to start and I was a nervous wreck. But, thankfully Stan let us use his house as a gathering for the family. Zavier's house was too far from which the funeral was being held anyway. "It's so nice to meet you Kaitlyn. We've heard so much about you. Sorry that we had to meet you under these circumstances." One of Zavier's female cousins said. I wasn't sure why he never brought none of his family members around. They all seemed very nice to me. Keith was there with me for support, however I introduced him as a dear friend because I didn't want the wrong idea about us in anyone's head. "I don't see why you lying to these folks. It's not like you know them for real anyway." Alivia said as she stood next to me looking at all these strangers. "I know. But how would it look if I just introduce Keith as my boyfriend at my fiancée funeral? I would look like a hoe." I whispered to her. She rolled her eyes at me because I knew she didn't care what nobody said about her and that's what I loved about her the most. She was very opened minded and stood up for herself. I had hoped to be like this one day. "Can I talk to you for a second?" Stan said as he grabbed my elbow. "Sure." I told him as we walked into the kitchen. Stan waited for the unwanted guest to leave before talking. "How are you holding up?" He asked me. "Well, so far I'm okay." I told him as I placed my hands on the counter. "Good. Anything you wanna talk about?" He asked me as he leaned up against the sink. "About?" I asked him as I tilted my head. "Anything?" He said again as he folded his arms. I told Stan that I didn't want to talk about Keith anymore and why I choose him. "That's not what I'm talking about." He told me. "Then what?" I asked him. "Keith said that last night you had a nightmare." Stan said. I bit my lip as I listened to Stan. I couldn't believe that Keith would go behind my back and tell Stan about this. "You do know that you are going to have to see a psychologist? This is unhealthy?" Stan advised as he walked over to me. "Hey, they're ready to head over to the funeral home." Keith said as he walked in. Stan quickly backed away as he didn't want Keith to get the wrong impression. "Stan, can we finish this later?" I told him as I wanted to talk to Keith alone. Stan held his hand up as he left the kitchen.

I asked Keith why he mentioned to Stan about last night. "Baby, I was worried. You wouldn't talk to me and whatever it was it scared the hell out of you." He said as he rubbed my face and tried to kiss me. "Did you tell him that you ate me out, too?" I said to him as I pushed him away. "No, baby. You won't let me all the way in. You didn't even want these people to know that we are together." He said as he pointed to the door. "That's not fair." I told him as I walked to the door. Alivia saw that my eyes were starting to tear up. "You okay?" She asked me as she looked back at Keith. "Yeah, it's just getting close to that time." I told her. I looked at Keith and told him that we would finish this conversation later as we were all getting ready for Zavier's funeral.

There was a lot faces that I knew and didn't know at the funeral, but it was a full house. Since I introduced Keith to everybody as a close dear friend it wasn't weird when he sat right next to me. After, the prayer it was time for me to say some kind words. I was nervous as hell, but was glad that the family asked if I would speak on behalf of all the family. "Now, we would like to ask Ms. Thomas to come and say a few words to the family." The pastor introduced me after he finished giving his prayer. I looked at Keith before getting up and he gave me the look of comfort. I placed my hand on Zavier's coffin before walking to the podium. "As I stand here today we celebrate the home going of Zavier Price. I would like to say a few kind words to the family. Zavier as we know, was very likeable and always willing to help. He could be found saving a life or making someone smile. He was always lending a helping hand at the hospital even if it meant that he hadn't been to sleep for twenty-four hours. Zavier was always searching or looking for medicines to cure the incurable. He wanted everyone to have a chance at happiness. Also, some of you may know that we were much in love and that we were supposed to be married next month. I loved Zavier and he was the perfect guy for me. I never imagined my life without him. He was always there and I didn't deserve him. He never asked me for much. He only wanted to be loved and in return..." I paused as I looked up and saw Zavier sitting next to Keith.

I could hear someone calling my name as I started opening my eyes. "Kaitlyn? Kaitlyn?" I could hear Stan saying. "Mmmm...." I was moaning as I was waking up. "Are you okay?" I heard Alivia asking from a far. "What happened?" I asked. "You passed out." Keith said as he was walking in with some water. I sat up to take a sip and noticed that the funeral home was empty. "Where is everybody?" I asked. "Well, after you passed out. They just kind of wrapped things up and just went on to the burial site." Keith told me as he sat down next to me. "What? Oh my God!" I said as I put my head down. "Don't worry about it. All of this was too soon after you got out of the hospital. Maybe you should go home and get some rest." Alivia told me. I nodded my head yes as I got up. "Come on I'll take you home." Stan announced as he grabbed my elbow. "I got her." Keith said as he moved Stan's hand from my elbow. "Don't touch me, man." Stan threatened Keith. "Well, don't put your hand on my woman." Keith snapped back. Stan. I asked them not to do this today because it wasn't the time nor was it the place. "Y'all stop. Not today. Keith, take her home. We'll come check on her later." Alivia said as she stood between Keith and Stan. I couldn't believe that they were acting like that on this particular day. But, most importantly this made the second time that I've seen Zavier since he's been dead.

CHAPTER 24

The next morning I was so tired because I couldn't sleep. I tossed and turned trying to figure out why I kept seeing Zavier after his death. "Do you wanna talk?" Keith asked as he sat up in the bed. "Yes, but I don't want it to push you away." I sat up too. "Baby, I'm here and I'm not going anywhere. "Well, the other day when I screamed, I saw Zavier, Then, I saw him again at the funeral. I don't know why I am seeing him and I don't know what it means." I revealed to Keith. "Aww baby. You just miss him that's all and its' okay to miss him. You didn't know that this was going to happen." Keith consoled me and placed my head on his chest. "I know, but I just got a feeling that seeing him has a meaning that I'm just not seeing right now." I told Keith as I looked into his eyes. He looked back into mine and kissed me. "Come here." Keith said as he placed his hands on my face to kiss me again. "What do you want to do today?" Keith asked me. "Hold that thought." I told Keith as I sent Alivia and Stan a text letting them know that they can go back home. "Will you go somewhere with me?" I asked "Of course. Where baby?" He asked me. "I can't tell you right now, but I promise that I will explain it to you later." I told him as I kissed him. I didn't want him to know that I was planning to take him to the asylum, but I knew that talking to a psychiatrist was the only way that I would get better.

"You sure you didn't want me to drive?" Keith asked me as he placed his hands on mine. "No, baby. I'm good." I told him as he kissed my hand. I hoped that Keith wouldn't get too freaked out when we arrived at the crazy house. Even though he's said that he would always be there for me I still couldn't tell him the whole truth and I guess that's why I couldn't tell him that I loved him yet. "Baby? Where are we?" Keith asked as we arrived at the gate. "Baby, for right now. Please don't ask any questions and I promise that I will explain everything to you later." I told him as I kissed him. He didn't argue with me as we drove in and I was glad because I was going to need all of my energy to talk to the doctor. The place hadn't changed one bit, even the same people worked there. "Excuse me is Doctor Marshall available?" I asked the nurse at the desk. "Ms. Thomas? What are you doing here?" She asked as she came around to hug me. "I just wanted to say, hi." I told her. "Well, let me just give him a call to see if he's available." She told me as she winked her eye at me and noticed Keith standing next to me. "Dr. Marshall you're needed in the front. Paging for Dr. Marshall." She said over the intercom. "He should be coming shortly." She advised. I thanked her as me and Keith went to have a seat to wait on him. "I will explain later, I promise." I told Keith as he looked around.

I saw the nurse pointing her finger towards me as she was looking up the hallway. "Ms. Thomas?" Dr. Marshall said as he walked towards me. "Hi, I was hoping that I could speak to you for a minute if you were available." I told him as I got up. "Sure, sure." He said as he led the way to his office. I asked Keith if he could wait and that I needed to talk to the doctor alone. I kissed him before leaving to let all the other nurses know that he was taken. I could tell that the Doctor was very surprised to see me because the last time that I was there I was making progress. "So, how can I help you Ms. Thomas?" The Doctor inquired. "Well, I confronted Eric about molesting me as a child. I found out that he was really my uncle and not my adoptive father. I cheated on my fiancée' and I buried him yesterday. So, now I keep seeing his dead body everywhere. I tried killing myself twice. Oh, and that white guy you see out there, that's who I cheated on him with and we're together now. Yep, that just about sums it up. Let me think? Nope! A woman keeps calling me saying that she's my birth mother when I was told that my mother was a drug addict and died of a drug overdose." I told Dr. Marshall as tears started rolling down my face. "Well, it seems like you had a breakthrough in ten minutes." The doctor told me as he looked at his watch. "So, what do I do? Because I'm lost." I told him as I wiped my eyes. "Ms. Thomas, I suggest that you get away from what is causing you problems. It may seem like you're running away, but if being here is causing all this hurt and pain then you will never get better." He told me as he was writing something down. "I have a colleague who lives in Atlanta that I want you to see. She's a great psychiatrist." He handed me the piece of paper. "I don't need to see anyone I have Keith." I told him as I gave him the paper back. "Ms. Thomas, if you didn't need help you wouldn't have come here. Obviously, you need help so please take her number and call her to schedule an appointment." H placed the paper in my hand. I didn't argue and just took the number from him. I was never good at admitting when I was wrong. "Call her." He yelled out as I was leaving his office. I nodded my head back as I was walked towards Keith. "Are you ready?" He asked me. "What would you say if I asked you to move with me?" I asked him as we were leaving. "Move in or move, like move away?" Keith asked for correction. "Move away, like maybe to Atlanta." I said. "Baby, I love you and I will follow you wherever you go. No matter the distance." He told me. "You will?" "Yes, no questions asked." He replied. Before I knew it I had told Keith that I loved him and saw the biggest smile on his face. "So, is it safe to say that we are moving?" He asked me as he started the car. "Yes, but I gotta do something first." I told him as we left the mental institution. I knew by now that Keith had figured out that I had been there before. He just didn't know if I was there as a child or if I was there as an adult, but he didn't ask any questions and that made me love him even more. Keith didn't care about my past, he was only concerned about our future together and I was looking forward to it, too.

After all the planning and digging information I was finally able to find the information pertaining to full ownership of the law firm. I wanted to make sure that when I left that no one would lose their job and that Eric lost all ownership to the firm. "Ms. Thomas, you understand that you will be selling us half of the firm which allows us to make certain decisions without contacting you?" The CEO of another law firm stated as he leaned back in his chair. "Yes, Mr. Brown, but if you would have fully read the contract and instead of just going by "word of mouth", you would've noticed that the only decisions that your company can make pertains to law cases. Your firm can not make any decisions that has to deal with the Thomas law firm and its inequalities." I told them as I closed my portfolio. "Smart woman." He commented. "Now if you gentlemen will excuse me, I have a plane to catch and it was a pleasure doing business with you." I got up from my chair to head for the elevators. My cell phone rang, but I didn't answer it because I knew it would hang up, so I waited until I got off. When the doors open I was looking down to see who I missed a call from when all of a sudden I fell force around my neck. "You filthy bitch. I'm gonna kill you." Eric had his hands tight around my neck. "Help! Help!" I said with a grasp. "Get off of her!" I heard Keith say as he pulled Eric off of me. I saw the anger in Keith's eyes as he was punching Eric in the face. It took three security men to pull him off Eric. "Call the police. Call the police. Do you know who I am?" Eric yelled as he wiped the blood from his nose. "That's not necessary. This man no longer has ownership to this company and I have the papers right here to prove it." I informed the security guards. They immediately walked over to me to check. "Sir, we're gonna have to ask you to leave." They told Eric as they grab his arm. "Get your hands off of me. This is my law firm. My granddaddy and my dad built this firm. This is in my blood." He told them as he snatched away. "Sir, we're only gonna ask you one more time to leave." They told them as they got on the radio to request assistance from the police. "Please, Eric. Go! You're making an ass out of yourself." I told him as Keith was holding me. "Look at you. You think you got this together. Don't you?" He said. "What the hell are you talking about now?' I asked him as he smell like he took a bath in scotch. "I'm not talking to you, you bitch. I'm talking to you." He said as he pointed to Keith. "Mr. Thomas, please don't talk to Kaitlyn in that way and I have no idea what you're talking about." Keith told him as we were trying to leave. "Sure you do, Mama's boy." Eric said. "Enough, Uncle Eric! Enough! You're not gonna do this to me anymore! You've hurt me for the last time, but not anymore. You ruined my childhood, you took the love of my life, and you took my mother, but no more. I'm in control and I don't want to see you ever again." I was adamant as me and Keith left the building. I didn't care that everyone was looking or that everyone heard because we were moving that day anyway. "Are you okay?" Keith asked as he opened my car door. "No?" I told him as I got in. "Thank you." Keith told me. "For what?" I asked him as I put my seat belt on. "Well, usually when I ask you that question you tell me that you're fine and I know you're not." He reminded. I kissed him and told him that I loved him.

"I love you too, and I am excited to start this journey with you." He told me and returned the kiss. "Yes, me too. But, we have one more stop to make." I told him as he put the car in reverse. It was a stop that I knew he was uncomfortable with making, but if we wanted this relationship to work it had to be done.

When we arrived at the grave site Keith was unsettle with the entire situation, but I told him that it would make me feel better. "I know that you think that this is silly, but even though he's gone in some way I feel like he can still see what's going on and I just need to tell him about us." I told Keith as I opened my door. "I know baby, it's just that I don't think that we're doing anything wrong." Keith told me as he turned the car off. "Will you get the flowers?" I asked him. He nodded his head yes and I waited for him in front of the car. I told him that it was polite to say a prayer and excuse me before walking onto a cemetery. "Why?" He asked. "Well, we meaning us black folks. We believe in being respectful to the spirit and body." I told him with a smile. "Yep, we cremate our loved ones." He answered with a laugh. We quickly stopped the jokes when we arrived at Zavier's head stone. "Hi, Zavier. I know that you are probably upset with me, but please don't be. Yes, I did cheat on you with Keith, but it was never on purpose. I guess I was just rushing into being with you and never just tried to focus on what I really wanted. I hope that you can forgive me and that you don't hate me." I told Zavier as I placed the flowers on the headstone. "Keith, you wanna say something?" I asked him as I wrapped my arm around his. "No, I don't know what to say.

I mean, I never really held a conversation with him." Keith told me as we stood there. "You're right. Rest, well Zavier." I blew him a kiss. I actually felt better after telling Zavier the truth even though it was to his grave. "Ready for the next chapter in our lives?" Keith asked me. "Of course, baby." I told him as I laid a kiss on his lips.

Carmen waited until she saw Kaitlyn leave before getting out to see Zavier. "We're here baby." She said as she was held a newborn baby girl. "She looks just like you." She said as she held the baby towards the headstone. "I love you and miss you, well, we miss you." She began to cry. "She thinks that this is over, but it's only the beginning. Kaitlyn Thomas is going to get what's coming to her. I promise you that as long as I am breathing that I will make her pay for taking you away from me." Carmen blamed Kaitlyn for her unhappy life and made plans to make her suffer just as much as she had. "Keith, will be first and then I will take care of her. Don't worry baby, your death will not be in vain." Carmen stated as she kissed his headstone. Carmen was on a journey of vengeance to ruin Kaitlyn life, and if she was going to be successful, she was going to need the help of Kaitlyn's past. She was going to seek the help from one of Kaitlyn's close relatives.